"I've come here today, Randy, prepared to make you a deal."

He raised his head and stared wide-eyed at her. "Short of saying *yes* to a divorce, I don't know what kind of a deal you can offer."

"Like I said, I still love you and don't want our marriage to end. So—here is the deal. I'll give you your divorce, uncontested, if you'll do one thing for me."

The look of relief in his eyes nearly made her cry. "What?"

"I want us to have one last Christmas together."

He shook his head slowly. "You mean you want me to move back in until after Christmas? No way! Leaving this time was hard enough. I'll not do it a second time!" He rose and moved around the desk toward the door.

"Your call, Randy. Do you want me to make a scene here in your office?"

He turned back to her. "Of course not!"

"Then sit down and listen to me."

JOYCE LIVINGSTON has done many things in her life (in addition to being a wife, mother of six, and grandmother to oodles of grandkids, all of whom she loves dearly), from being a television broadcaster for eighteen years, to lecturing and teaching on quilting and sewing, to writing magazine articles on a variety of subjects. She's danced with Lawrence Welk, ice-skated with a Chimpanzee, had bottles broken over her head by stuntmen, interviewed hundreds of celebrities and controversial figures, and done many other interesting and unusual things. But now, when she isn't off traveling to wonderful and exotic places as a part-time tour escort, her days are spent sitting in front of her computer, creating stories. She feels her writing is a ministry and a calling from God, and she hopes Heartsong readers will be touched and uplifted by what she writes. Joyce loves to hear from her readers and invites you to visit her on the Internet at: www.joycelivingston.com

Books by Joyce Livingston

HEARTSONG PRESENTS
HP353—Ice Castle
HP382—The Bride Wore Boots
HP437—Northern Exposure
HP482—Hand Quilted with Love
HP516—Lucy's Quilt
HP521—Be My Valentine
HP546—Love Is Kind
HP566—The Baby Quilt
HP578—The Birthday Wish
HP602—Dandelion Bride

Don't miss out on any of our super romances. Write to us at the following address for information on our newest releases and club information.

Heartsong Presents Readers' Service
PO Box 719
Uhrichsville, OH 44683

Or visit www.heartsongpresents.com

One Last Christmas

Joyce Livingston

Heartsong Presents

I dedicate this book to all of you who are struggling to keep your marriage together. I was eighteen when Don and I were married (a mere child!), standing at that altar with my head in the clouds, smiling and repeating those vows without fully realizing the lifetime commitment I was making. However, six children and oodles of grandchildren later, I'm still happily married to the same godly man. If you learn one lesson from this book, may it be this: Love thrives in the face of all life's hazards, except one. Neglect.

A note from the Author:
I love to hear from my readers! You may correspond with me by writing:

> **Joyce Livingston**
> **Author Relations**
> **PO Box 719**
> **Uhrichsville, OH 44683**

ISBN 1-59310-242-9

ONE LAST CHRISTMAS

Our mission is to publish and distribute inspirational products offering exceptional value and biblical encouragement to the masses.

All Scripture quotations are taken from the King James Version of the Bible.

All of the characters and events in this book are fictitious. Any resemblance to actual persons, living or dead, or to actual events is purely coincidental.

PRINTED IN THE U.S.A.

Or check out our Web site at www.heartsongpresents.com

one

Sylvia Benson hid behind the potted palm and tried to remain calm. Her intense gaze riveted on the man and woman seated at a table for two in the far corner of Dallas's trendy Fountain Place Avanti Restaurant. Hadn't her husband told her he would be having lunch with one of his key advertisers today? *That's no advertising client! That's Chatalaine Vicker, the woman who writes the society column for his newspaper. I'd recognize that gorgeous face and body anywhere. What is he doing here with her?*

"More coffee, ladies?"

Caught up in staring at the blond beauty seated across from her husband, Sylvia hadn't even noticed the waiter standing by their table, coffeepot in hand. She flinched, then covered her cup. "None for me, thanks."

The other women at the table, all friends from her church, bobbed their heads at the man without even a pause in their conversation.

Still trying to remain inconspicuous, Sylvia shifted her position slightly. Making sure the potted palm shielded her, she took another look at the pair in the corner. Surely, Randy hadn't lied to her. Not her Randy. Although he *had* been spending more time than usual at the *Dallas Times* office, occasionally even working weekends. *Come on, Sylvia, give that husband of yours the benefit of the doubt*, she told herself as she stared at them. *Maybe his client had to cancel their luncheon appointment at the last minute*. But even if that were true, what would Randy be doing with Chatalaine? And why hadn't he told her he would be free for lunch? After all, she was his wife.

If he had wanted someone to go to lunch with him, she could have cancelled her luncheon appointment with her friends.

She leaned back in her chair and tried to shake off her suspicions. *It's probably all perfectly innocent, and I'm making something out of nothing. Business associates have lunch together all the time. Maybe they're discussing Chatalaine's column. After all, Randy is the* Times's *managing editor.*

"What *are* you looking at, Sylvia?"

Sylvia turned quickly toward the question and found her friend, Sally, staring at her. "Ah, nothing. Just thought I recognized someone."

Sally rose, placed her napkin on the table, and picked up her purse. "I'm going to the ladies' room. Anyone want to go with me?"

Without missing a beat in their conversation, Denise and Martha rose and headed for the ladies' room, still talking.

Sally gave a slight giggle. "You're not coming?"

"No, I'll wait here. You go on."

"Don't let that waiter get away if he comes with the dessert cart while we're gone," Sally said with a mischievous lilt. "I need chocolate."

Sylvia snickered. "You're terrible!"

She waited until her friends were out of sight, then turned and tipped her head slightly, parting the palm fronds again and peering through them. What she observed went a long way toward fueling her suspicions. The two were talking and giggling like two teenagers. *If this is supposed to be a business luncheon, those two are enjoying themselves entirely too much! Maybe I should just march right over there and confront them, ask them what they're doing together, and see what kind of an explanation I get.*

However, she didn't. Her pride would not allow it. Instead, she decided to wait until later, when she and Randy were alone. She sat there quietly, her nerves French-braiding themselves while all sorts of scenarios played themselves out in her mind. She flinched when the waiter filled her water glass, his close proximity pulling her out of her thoughts.

"Would you like to see the dessert cart, ma'am?"

"Ah—in a minute maybe." She motioned toward the hallway off to the left. "As soon as my friends come back from the ladies' room."

When he nodded and moved away, Sylvia twisted in the chair, unable to resist another peek. Randy was standing beside Chatalaine now, extending his hand to assist her as she rose. How long had it been since he had done that for her? Things were not looking good.

From behind her potted palm camouflage, she watched the attractive couple move across the restaurant toward the exit. After giving them enough time to reach the parking lot, she signaled the waiter and asked for her check.

I wonder how long this has been going on? She drummed her fingers on the table. *You're making too much of this, Sylvia. There's probably a perfectly reasonable explanation as to why your Randy and that woman had lunch together.* She dabbed at her misty eyes with a tissue. *If you confront Randy about this now, you may be sorry. Tomorrow is Thanksgiving, and the children will all be home. You don't want to ruin Thanksgiving for your family with your unconfirmed suspicions, do you? At least wait until DeeDee and Aaron go back to college. Then, if you still think there may be something going on between your husband and that woman, you can ask him.*

The plan sounded logical. But, at this minute, she felt anything *but* logical. Both she and Randy were Christians. Randy would never go against the commitments they had both made to God on their wedding day. Or would he? Had his faith slipped, and she had been so busy, she hadn't even realized it?

"He hasn't brought the dessert cart yet?" Sally slipped into the chair, eyeing Sylvia with a grin.

Sylvia scooted her chair back and placed her napkin on the table. "I—I really need to go home."

Sally's brow creased. "Go? You and I haven't even had time for a little girl talk. What's your rush? I thought you said you didn't have any plans for this afternoon."

Sylvia reached for her purse, pulled out a couple of dollar bills, and dropped them on the table beside her plate. "I'm sorry, Sally. We'll talk more next time we have lunch. I've developed a splitting headache."

Sally gave her a slight giggle. "Hey, that's the line we use with our husbands, not our girlfriends."

Sylvia frowned as her hand rose to finger her temple. "I'm really sorry, Sally. I hate to duck out on you like this, but I need to get home, take something for this headache, and lie down. Please tell Denise and Martha good-bye for me." She didn't have a headache before seeing Randy with that woman, but witnessing them together—after he had told her he was meeting with a client—had brought on a doozy.

Sally's face sobered. "Oh, sweetie, I'm sorry, I was only kidding. Do you feel like driving home by yourself?"

"Sure, I'll be fine. Don't worry about me." *Actually, I'm miserable!* Though Sally was one of her best friends, she simply could not reveal her unproven suspicions about her husband.

When he came home from his office, it was all Sylvia could do to keep from screaming out at Randy and asking him about his lunch with Chatalaine. But for the sake of the twins, DeeDee and Aaron, who had arrived home from college that afternoon, she kept quiet, pasting on a smile and brooding within herself. She had a difficult time even looking at Randy.

She waited expectantly at bedtime, hoping he would mention it. But he didn't. Even when she asked him how his day went, he simply replied, "Fine. Routine, just like any other day." Then he crawled into bed and turned away from her.

Okay, if that's the way you want it! Don't tell me. She yanked the quilt up over her head and gritted her teeth to keep from screaming at him, telling him she had seen the two of them having a cozy lunch together.

After a sleepless night, she crawled out of bed earlier than she'd intended and began to go mechanically through the tasks of baking the turkey and preparing the rest of their very traditional meal. Her mind still on the events of yesterday, she took out her anger and frustration on the celery stalks and onions as she mercilessly chopped them up on the cutting block.

Randy came into the kitchen about eight, his usual pleasant self. He rousted Aaron and DeeDee and even teased Sylvia about the bag of giblets she'd left in the turkey she'd prepared for their first Thanksgiving together as husband and wife. About eleven o'clock, their oldest son, Buck, and his wife, Shonna, arrived, bringing two beautiful pecan pies Shonna had baked. Randy greeted them warmly, then dragged both Buck and Aaron into the den to watch a football game while the three women finished setting the table.

"Is something wrong?" Shonna stared at her mother-in-law while removing the gravy boat from the china cabinet. "You're pretty quiet this morning."

DeeDee nodded her head in agreement. "Yeah, Mom, I noticed that, too."

Is it that obvious? "I'm fine. Just had a hard time getting to sleep last night." Sylvia forced a smile. It was nice having Shonna and DeeDee there to help her. "Maybe we'd better use that big serving bowl, DeeDee. Hand it to me, would you, please?"

By one o'clock, the Benson family gathered around the lovely table for their Thanksgiving feast. With everyone holding hands, Randy led in prayer. As he did at every Thanksgiving, he thanked God for their food, for the willing hands that prepared it, and for their family seated at the table. Sylvia found it difficult to keep her mind on his words. All she could think about was her husband having lunch with that gorgeous blond. Was this all for show? Inside, was Randy wishing he could be spending Thanksgiving Day with Chatalaine?

After he had consumed the last crumb of pie on his overloaded dessert plate, Randy pushed back from the table and linked his fingers over his abdomen. "Great Thanksgiving dinner, hon. The turkey was nice and moist, just the way I like it. As usual, you've outdone yourself." With a tilt of his head, he gave her a slightly twisted smile. "If my mother was alive, she would agree, and you know how picky she was."

"Thanks. That's quite a compliment." Sylvia nervously shifted the salt and pepper shakers, finally placing them on either side of the antique sugar bowl, a prize possession that had belonged to her mother-in-law. *Oh, Randy, how I hope I'm wrong! I know we haven't had much to do with each other these past few years, but surely that didn't drive you into another woman's arms.*

"Sorry, Mom. DeeDee and I have to go." Aaron tossed his napkin onto the table and nodded to his sister.

"You *have* to go this early?" Sylvia dabbed at her mouth with her napkin. "You just got here yesterday."

The good-looking young man, who looked so much like his father, gave her a quick, affectionate peck on the cheek. "I know. But you knew we'd planned to get back to school right after our meal. DeeDee and I promised we'd help our youth director with the lock-in tonight, and we've got a ton of stuff to do to get the fellowship hall ready before the kids get there."

"Great dinner, Mom." DeeDee pushed back from the table. "I hate to run and leave you and Shonna with the dishes, but if we don't leave now, we won't make it."

Sylvia rose and walked to the door with her children, with Randy following close behind. "I'm glad you're both active in the church you attend, but isn't there someone else who could—"

"Hey, DeeDee and I are the lucky ones. Most college students don't live within driving distance of their homes. Besides, we have to get back to our jobs." Aaron threw a playful punch at his father's stomach. "Maybe this old man'll help you with the dishes."

Randy let out an exaggerated "ugh" before wrapping his arm around his son's shoulders and pulling him close. "I'm counting on the two of you taking care of each other."

Buck shook hands with his brother, then kissed his little sister's cheek. "Yeah, Aaron, watch after this cute freshman. I know how those college boys can be. I was one of them once," he added with a chuckle. "Come to think of it, maybe I'd better have DeeDee keep an eye on you since you're a freshman, too."

Both Aaron and DeeDee kissed Shonna, then picked up their backpacks from the hall bench and headed for the door.

Sylvia followed them, then kissed each one on the cheek, giving them a hug as she struggled to hold back her tears. "I really hate to see you leave, but I'm so thankful the two of you get home as often as you do. It's just that—"

Grinning, Aaron tapped the tip of his mother's nose. "I know. You love us."

"We love you, too, Mom." DeeDee nudged her father with her hip. "You, too, Dad."

The two stood in the open doorway waving as their two precious children crawled into Aaron's beat-up old van. "Promise you'll drive carefully!" Sylvia called after them before its door slid closed.

"We gotta go, too, Mom." Buck motioned his wife toward the door. "Shonna's parents are expecting us. Can you believe we're gonna eat two Thanksgiving dinners today, and her mom's nearly as good a cook as you?"

Shonna rolled her eyes and pelted her husband with a pillow from the sofa. "Don't let my mom hear you say that, if you expect to win brownie points with her."

Randy and Sylvia watched until Buck's car was out of sight before shutting the door. For the first time since the restaurant incident, she was alone with her husband, and she felt as nervous as a tightrope walker wearing hiking boots.

Randy moved through the family room after grabbing the heavy Thanksgiving edition of the newspaper that lay on the hall table. "I wish the kids hadn't had to rush off. I really miss them and all the noise they make when they're here."

Sylvia followed, scooping up the pillow Shonna had tossed at Buck. With an audible sigh, she placed it back in its proper place on the sofa. "I like the kind of Thanksgivings we used to have, before they grew up. Thanksgivings where we spent the entire day together, just enjoying one another's company." She allowed the corners of her mouth to curl up slightly and managed a nervous chuckle. "I didn't even mind you and the boys spending most of the afternoon in front of the TV watching football."

He gave her another twisted smile; this one she did not understand. Was his demeanor sending up bells of alarm? Signals he hoped she would catch? He seemed nervous, too. Ill at ease. Was he going to tell her that he, also, had to rush off? Was he planning to spend the rest of the day with his girlfriend, now that their children had gone? *Girlfriend?* That word struck horror in her heart and made her lightheaded.

"Those were good days, weren't they?" Randy pulled the newspaper from its bright orange plastic wrapper, tossed it into his recliner chair, then moved into the dining room. As he stared at the table, almost robotically he reached for the salt and pepper shakers and placed them on a tray. "But things change, Syl. People change. Life changes."

What does that mean? She began adding cups and saucers to the tray, eyeing him suspiciously. "My, but you're philosophical today."

Randy nodded but did not comment and continued to add things to the tray. His silence made her edgy. She wanted to reach out and shake him. *Say something. Tell me about your lunch with Chatalaine! Give me some excuse I can believe!* "Would you like another sliver of pumpkin pie?" she asked, biting her tongue to keep from saying something she might later regret. *What is it the scripture says? A tiny spark can ignite a forest fire?*

"No, thanks. It was great, but I'm full." He picked up the tray and headed for the kitchen.

"More coffee? I think there's still some left in the pot." She quickly gathered up the remaining silverware and followed.

"I've had plenty." He placed the tray on the counter, then sat down at the table. "Want me to help you with the dishes?"

Sylvia glanced up at the big, round clock on the kitchen wall. The one Randy had given her for Christmas two years ago. An artist friend of his had painted the words, *Sylvia's Kitchen*, across the face in bold letters and had even added a tiny picture of her where the twelve should've been. She had cried with joy at the thoughtful gift. Even now, with the tenseness she felt between them, just looking at the clock brought a warm feeling to her heart. "No football on TV?"

He shrugged. "I don't want to watch TV."

She pasted on a smile and counted his options on her fingers. "You don't want pie. You don't want coffee. You don't want to watch the game. But you want to help me with the dishes?"

Randy straightened in his chair and placed both palms flat on the table in front of him, his gaze locking with hers. "What I really want—" He paused and swallowed hard. "Is— is a divorce!"

two

Sylvia's breath caught in her throat. All she could do was stare at him in disbelief. Her heart raced and thundered against her chest. *This can't be happening! Please, God, tell me I'm dreaming!*

"I—I didn't want to hurt you, Syl. But I couldn't think of another way to tell you other than just blurting it out like that. I've been trying to tell you for weeks."

He reached for her hand, but she quickly withdrew it and linked her fingers together, dipping her head and turning away from him. She could not bring herself to look at him. Not the way she was feeling. Her legs wobbled beneath her and, afraid they might not hold her up a second longer, she clutched onto the cabinet. *So, what I witnessed in the restaurant and hoped was an innocent lunch was exactly what I suspected? You do have a girlfriend!*

She found herself anchored to the spot—speechless. She had been concerned there was something going on between Randy and Chatalaine. But had it gone this far? *No! Please, God. No!*

"Say something, Syl. Don't just stand there. I hate myself for telling you like this—"

"*You* hate yourself?" She sank onto the kitchen stool and looked up slowly, her shock turning to anger as her heart pounded wildly and her stomach began to lurch. "You can't begin to imagine the feelings of hurt and resentment welling up inside me! Why, Randy? Why? Has our married life been that bad?"

He stood awkwardly and began pacing about the room, his fingers combing through his distinguished-looking graying temples. "Like I said, Syl. Life changes. We change."

Sylvia spun around on the seat. Fear, anger, betrayal bit at her heart, and it felt like a wad in her chest. Her fingers clutched the stool's high back for both support and stability. "Of course, things change! The raising of our three children has taken most of my time, while you've been building your career at the newspaper! But our kids are gone now. Out on their own. We finally have the time for ourselves we've always talked about! It's our time now! Yours and mine! Why would you even think about a divorce?" *Say it, Randy. Be a big enough man to tell me you're leaving me for a younger woman!*

He stopped pacing and stood directly in front of her. The pale blue eyes she had always loved, now a cold, icy gray—eyes she barely recognized. He hesitated for what seemed an eternity, then turned away as if to avoid the sight of her. "Our marriage died a long time ago. Have you been so blind you haven't noticed?"

"Have *I* been so blind? Don't try to blame this on me, Randy Benson!" Sylvia felt like she had been sucker punched in the stomach as his words assaulted her and threshed away at her brain. "How stupid do you think I am? You're leaving me for that Chatalaine woman, aren't you?"

He flinched, and she could see he was startled by her mention of the woman's name. "Chatalaine? What made you say that?"

"I—I saw the two of you together." Why couldn't she cry? She wanted to cry, but the tears would not come. It almost seemed as if she were standing outside her body, watching this dreadful scene happen to someone else. "Yo–you've been having an—"

"Me? Having an affair?" He turned and grabbed onto the back of her chair. "I resent that accusation, Syl! How dare you even consider such a thing?"

She leaped to her feet and stood toe-to-toe with him. She wanted him to look at her when he told her his dirty little secrets. "Come on, Randy. Tell me. Admit to your little trysts!"

"Are you crazy? I have no idea what you're talking about."

She felt him cringe as her hands cupped his biceps and her fingers dug into his flesh. "You're a Christian, Randy! How could you?"

"Look, Syl, I'm sure you don't want to hear this, but the two of us—you and I alone—are responsible for the breakup of this marriage. I should have put my foot down—"

She felt the hair stand up on her arms. "Put your foot down? Exactly what do you mean by that?"

He stared at the floor. "Perhaps that was a poor choice of words. What I meant was—" He stopped, as if wanting to make sure his words came out right this time. "I—I should have complained more, instead of holding things back. Keeping things inside."

"Things? What kind of things?"

He gave a defeated shrug. "You were so busy with the kids, you never had time for me. I needed you, Syl, but you shut me out."

"I didn't shut you out, Randy. You were never here long enough to be shut out, or have you forgotten all the days, nights, and weekends you spent at the newspaper? What about the times *I* needed *you*?" she shot back defensively.

"I'd much rather have been at home like you, but as the breadwinner of this family, I didn't have that luxury."

"Oh, and I did have that luxury? Staying home with crying babies, doing a myriad of laundry each week, cooking countless meals, cleaning the house so things would look nice for you when you came home?" She could not remember the last time she had been so angry.

"I didn't want things to turn out like this. I—"

"Don't tell me the devil made you do it!" she shot out at him, suddenly wanting to hurt him as he was hurting her. He tried to back away, but she clung tightly to his arms and would not allow it.

"Syl, don't. You're only making this harder for both of us."

"Don't what? Cry? Scream? Get mad? You don't think you deserve to be screamed at? After what you've just said?" She continued to hold onto him, wanting him to feel her anger and frustration, to see it on her face. She wanted him to sense her fury. To feel her angst. What do you say to a man who just asked you for a divorce, when all this time you've had no idea he's been cheating on you?

He gave her a disgruntled snort. "If I didn't know better, I'd say you were jealous, but I don't think you care enough to be jealous."

She jammed her hand onto her hip. "Oh? Does that question mean I have a reason to be jealous?"

"Of course not. I was referring to your attitude."

She continued to hold tightly to his arms, sure that if she ever let him go, it would be for good. She could not bear the idea of life without him. She inhaled a deep breath and let it out slowly, begging God to give her the right words to say and the right way to react, to make her beloved husband come to his senses. Why didn't he come right out and tell her about Chatalaine? That she was the real reason he wanted out?

After an interminable silence, she willed herself to calm down and said, trying to mask her disillusionment, "We can't do this, Randy. Divorce is not an option. We've both invested way too much in this marriage to give up on it now. Please, don't do anything you'll regret later. Have you prayed about this?"

He gently pried her fingers from her arm and walked away, turning when he reached the door to the hallway. "My mind is made up, Syl. For weeks, I have been trying to muster up the courage to do this. Now that I have finally said it, I am going to go through with it. You'll survive. I will continue to provide for you. I—I just want out."

"Would you pray with me about it?" she asked in desperation.

He shook his head. "No."

"Is Chatalaine married?"

"What's she got to do with this?"

His puzzled look infuriated her.

"You thought I didn't know your dirty little secret, didn't you?" she spat back, glowering at him.

"What secret?"

She felt her nostrils flare and her heart palpitate. "Come on, Randy, tell me about your lunch with your *client*! The one with the bleached blond hair and long, shapely legs that go up to her armpits. Did you make a sale? Is your social columnist going to purchase advertising with your precious newspaper because of your charms and your flawless sales pitch?"

He crossed the room quickly and grabbed onto her wrist, his nose close to hers. "Look, Syl. I have no idea what you're talking about. Yes, I had lunch with Chatalaine. A perfectly innocent lunch. The client called on my cell phone just before I reached the restaurant and said he couldn't make it. Since her column runs on the front page of that section and I was planning to pitch a succession of ads in the Dallas Life Section, I thought it would be helpful to have Chatalaine there." He turned loose and stepped back with a shake of his head. "You're barking up the wrong tree if you're trying to accuse me of being unfaithful."

Like she always did when she was upset, Sylvia gnawed nervously on her lower lip, biting back words she knew she would be sorry for later if they escaped. *Is it possible I could have been wrong? Was it an innocent lunch like he said?*

"Face it, Syl. Another woman didn't break up our marriage.

It's been dying for years, and we've both contributed to its death by ignoring it. I've realized it for some time. Maybe, if you were honest with yourself, you'd admit it, too. All we've been doing is marking time."

Divorce? That meant Randy would be leaving. She gasped at the paralyzing thought. "You're—you're not moving out, are you? Christmas is coming and the whole family will be—"

"There'll never be a good time. If there was, I'd have left months ago." He backed toward the hall again, as if wanting to put distance between the two of them, to pull away from her and all she represented.

This may be your only chance to try to save your marriage, she cautioned herself as she stared at the only man she'd ever loved. *Be careful what you say. Words, once said, can never be taken back.* "Please, Randy," she began, trying to add a softness to her voice when, inside, a storm was raging. "Give our marriage another chance. Just tell me what I'm doing wrong, and I'll change. I don't want you to leave. I—I love you!"

He did not look up. "I've worked long, hard hours for this family; now it's time for me. I'm going to get out and enjoy myself. Do some things I've put off for way too long."

His indifference broke her heart. "You could still do those things—"

"No." Keeping his gaze away from her face, he frowned and pursed his lips. "It's too late, Syl. I'm moving out. I packed up most of my personal things this morning while you were in the kitchen. I'll come back for the rest later."

Heaviness pressed against her heart and made it difficult to speak. "Yo–you're moving in with that woman?"

He gave her a look of annoyance. "No! Haven't you heard a word I've said?"

She rushed toward him and grabbed onto his arm, her fingernails nearly piercing the flesh. "You can't go! I won't let you!"

He pulled her hand away and rubbed at the red marks on his arm. "Hurting you is the last thing I wanted to do, Syl, but I can't keep living like this. The only fair way was to tell you this so we could both get on with our lives."

"Get *on* with our lives? How can I live without you, Randy? You expect me to believe you're not leaving me for another woman? Not for Chatalaine?"

His doubled up fist hit the palm of his other hand as his face filled with anger. "How many times do I have to tell you, Syl? There *is* no other woman! My lunch with Chatalaine was a legitimate, business-related luncheon, and I resent the idea that you would even think I'm cheating on you! Whatever happened to trust?"

"Trust? You ask *me* about trust?" Seeing the strange look in his eyes made her wonder at his words. Was that look guilt? Was he using anger and indignation to cover up his philandering? "Can you look me in the eye, Randy, and tell me this was the first time you and that woman have had lunch together?"

He did not have to answer. His face told it all.

"We've had lunch a few times but only to discuss her column—and those were on days you cancelled on me at the last minute because you were called to serve on some committee at the church or had to take a casserole to a sick person. You were always doing something for someone else when I needed you. Don't try to blame this on Chatalaine and a few business lunches."

Why hadn't she kept her mouth shut? "You're—you're really going through with this? Couldn't we maybe just have a separation for a while, so you can make sure you really want this before you take legal action?"

He gave her a flip of his hand. "A separation? Why? We've been living separate lives for years. I can't even remember the last time we—" He stopped midsentence.

His words hurt, and as badly as she hated to admit it, he was right. They'd both been so busy; they'd either been dead tired at the end of the day, she'd had one of her migraine headaches, or one of them had gone to bed early. But weren't there other ways of expressing your love other than physical? She had always thought taking good care of their children had been an act of love toward Randy. Keeping his house in perfect order and making sure his shirts were starched and ironed the way he liked them, to her, spoke of her love and adoration. Having good, nourishing meals on the table—sometimes having to reheat them because he got home late—all of those things and dozens of others were ways of saying *I love you*, weren't they?

"The children will have to be told," he said so matter-of-factly it only added to her already frazzled nerves.

She stepped back and crossed her arms over her chest, staring at him and seeing a stranger. "This is your party, Randy. Are you going to do the gentlemanly thing and tell them, or are you going to wait and let them find out for themselves? They'll hate you, you know."

"I'm hoping they won't hate me."

"They will. Our sons have always looked up to you as their role model. You've certainly fallen off that pedestal."

"I'll tell them," he murmured softly.

Sylvia pushed past him, rushed into the family room, afraid if she stood on her feet another minute she'd collapse.

Randy followed.

She shrugged and released a hefty sigh. "They say the wife is always the last to know. I guess that's because loving wives like me trust their husbands." She sat down quickly on the cushy green leather sofa, the one the two of them had selected together to commemorate their twentieth anniversary, and rubbed her hands over its smooth surface. "You certainly had me fooled. I thought we were getting along fine. I loved our life together."

He moved to the matching recliner, the roomier one they had specialty-ordered as his chair. But Sylvia reached out her hand and hollered, "Stop!"

He abruptly stepped to one side, giving her a puzzled look. "Stop what?"

She blinked her tear-filled eyes and pointed her finger at him defiantly. "Don't you dare sit in that chair! That chair is reserved for the head of this house. That wonderful, godly man I married. That description no longer fits you!"

Randy scooted over to a small, upholstered chair. "How about here?"

She nodded, feeling a bit chagrined, but he had to face reality. The breaking up of their marriage was something *he* wanted, not her.

Neither spoke for several minutes.

"I do love you, you know," she said finally, the tears now beginning to flow down her cheeks unashamedly. "I've always loved you. There's never been anyone else. Only you. Even if I haven't shown it much."

Randy hung his head and smoothed at the arm cover on the club chair. "I loved you, too, but—"

"But you no longer love me? Is that it?"

"I guess."

She glared at him, his answers not at all what she wanted to hear. "For a man who just asked his wife of twenty-five years for a divorce, you sure do a lot of guessing! Tell me outright, Randy. Do you or do you not love me?"

"I love you as the mother of my children," he said weakly, "and I care about you."

She bit at her lip until it hurt. "But you no longer love me as your wife? Your soul mate? Your lover? Is that the reason you never hug me anymore? Or touch me like you used to? Is that what you're saying?"

"I gu—yes."

"When did you make this amazing discovery? Before or after that woman came into your life?" She rose slowly, crossed the room, and knelt beside him. She had to find a way to make him change his mind. "Look into my eyes, Randy. See the pain I'm feeling. Think about the times we've shared together over the past twenty-five years—times both good and bad. Think about the struggles we've gone through together. And, yes, think about the times we've expressed our love for one another, though they may have been few lately. Then tell me. Tell me you don't love me anymore. Say the words. Convince me."

His gaze went to his lap, and for long moments, he stared at his hands, methodically checking one fingernail at a time before he looked up at her. "I think whatever love I felt for you is gone, Syl, and has been for some time."

Those words cut so deeply, Sylvia was sure they had actually punctured her flesh and her blood was pouring from the cuts they had inflicted. Slowly, she stood and pulled herself up tall. She had to be strong even though her heart was breaking. Strong for herself and strong for her family, what there was left of it.

"If you're sure that's the way you feel and you're not willing to give our marriage another chance, then go, Randy. Go now. Give up the life the two of us made together. Give up your children, your home. Just remember, it was you who broke up this family. I have God to turn to, but I doubt very seriously He'll want to hear from you, unless it's to ask His forgiveness for what you're doing." She moved quickly to the double glass doors leading onto the patio, sliding one side open before she turned to face him again, her lips trembling. "It's your decision."

Without a word, Randy stood, started to say something but didn't, then hesitantly moved through the door and onto the porch.

Sylvia slid the door closed behind him and twisted the lock, shutting it on twenty-five years of marriage.

three

Sylvia rushed to the narrow window beside the front door and pulled back the drapery just far enough to be able to watch Randy as he walked to his car, climbed in, started the engine, and drove away without even a backward glance. It was as though her very life ended with his departure. She wanted to pray, to ask God to bring her husband back to her, but the words would not come. It seemed even God had walked out on her. How could He have let this happen to their marriage?

Now what? Should she cry? No, she was too mad to cry. Throw things? Call the pastor? Go to bed and pull the covers over her head?

In robotic fashion, too numb to do anything, she moved to his recliner where the holiday edition of the *Dallas Times* still lay unrolled. How many times had she actually read the society column in the "Dallas Life" section? Probably not more than a dozen in all the years Randy had worked for the newspaper. Although her husband was constantly involved with community activities since he had been appointed managing editor, they rarely attended social functions together.

Maybe we should have, she told herself numbly as she lugged the heavy newspaper into the kitchen and poured herself that last cup of coffee before unplugging the pot. *Maybe that's one of the areas of Randy's life where I should have been more involved.* She tried to remember. *Did he ever ask me to go to one of those functions and I refused? Unfortunately, now that I think about it, he did. A number of times. But I had no interest in such things, and he never pressed the issue when I said no. If he felt they were important, he should have mentioned it instead of going on alone.* Her cup hit the table with a loud clunk, spattering coffee over the gingham placemat. *He went on without me!* That realization made her insides quiver. *I should have been with him! I should have bought that new dress he suggested and gone along, despite my lack of interest! For Randy's sake! Have I actually taken him for granted all these years, like he said? Is it my fault he's turned to someone else?*

She grabbed the dishrag from the sink and dabbed at the spilled coffee before settling down in the chair with the newspaper. Before she had seen her with Randy, she had never given much thought to Chatalaine. To her, the woman was just one of the many employees who worked for him. A columnist. Nothing more.

Until now.

Now, she was reasonably sure Chatalaine Vicker was the reason their marriage was about to end.

Sylvia thumbed through the paper, discarding section after section, until she came to the one marked "Dallas Life." There, glaring out at her with what she now perceived as a smirk instead of a smile, was the lovely, young face of Chatalaine Vicker, her nemesis.

Suddenly, feelings and emotions hitherto foreign to Sylvia came racing to the surface, and she wanted to go to that woman and scratch her eyes out. The woman who apparently wanted her husband and was more than likely willing to do whatever it took to get him. Did Randy really expect her to believe he wanted to leave her simply to find himself?

Blinking hard and trying to focus her eyes through the tears and terror she felt, she looked at the photograph again. She had to admit the woman was beautiful. The colorful picture, taking up a good portion of the first two columns, showed a full-length, enticingly posed view of Chatalaine's gorgeous, willowy figure as she stood leaning against a wall, her long arms crossed over her chest, a captivating smile adorning her perfectly made-up face. Even her name looked captivating, spread across the top of the page in an elegant, sprawling script. *What woman has a name like Chatalaine?*

Sylvia looked from the picture, to the half-empty cup of coffee, back to the picture, and back to the cup again. "Here's to you, you home wrecker!" she told the print version of her adversary as she slowly poured the remaining hot, black coffee over Chatalaine's face and body. "You wanted him. It looks like you got him! And I never even knew we were competing."

The ringing of the phone startled her, and the cup fell from her hands as she leaped to answer it, spilling the last few drops of coffee onto the floor. *Oh, dear God, let it be Randy calling to tell me it was all a joke!* "Hello!" she said eagerly into the phone, smiling and brushing away a tear.

"Hi. Just wanted to wish you a happy Thanksgiving."

She recognized the voice immediately. It was their pastor's wife, who was also her best friend. Sylvia's heart sank. "Hi, Jen."

"Hey, you don't sound so good. Are you coming down with a cold? Your voice sounds husky."

I can't tell her. Not yet. Not until I've had a chance to think this through. Do I want my church friends to know my husband has just asked me for a divorce? "May—maybe I am. I'm really not feeling up to par." She struggled to keep her words even, free of the raging emotions whirling inside her, when what she really wanted to do was cry out for sympathy. If she felt she could tell anyone, it would be Jen. But not now. Not yet.

"So? Is your family gathered around the TV set watching the game like my family is?"

Sylvia swallowed at the lump in her throat that nearly gagged her. Oh, how she wished they were in front of the TV. "No, DeeDee and Aaron both had to go back to college, to help out with the youth lock-in, and Buck and Shonna are spending the rest of the day with her parents."

"I'll bet Randy is glued to the set. I think the teams are tied. There's so much whooping and hollering going on in the other room, I can barely hear you."

"Ah—no. Randy isn't here. He—he had to—ah to go down to the newspaper office." Although Sylvia had worked hard all her life at either telling the truth or just remaining silent, she felt she had to lie to protect Randy, still hoping he would change his mind and come home.

"On a holiday? Isn't that asking a bit much of the guy?"

"Ah—that's what happens—when you're the managing editor, I guess."

"Poor boy. His body may be at the paper, but I'll bet his mind is wishing he was there with you."

"I hope so." This time Sylvia's words were honest. She did hope he was wishing he was there with her, but after his dogged determination to get away from her, she doubted it."

"Well, that's all I called you for. To wish you a happy Thanksgiving and tell you that we love the two of you. So many folks in our congregation are experiencing marital troubles. It's refreshing to talk to someone who has accomplished twenty-five years of marital bliss. You two are a real inspiration to the rest of us."

Sylvia felt sick to her stomach as she clung to the phone with clammy hands, feeling like an imposter. "Ha–happy Thanksgiving to you, too, Jen. Thanks for calling."

After pressing the OFF button and placing the phone back on the table, she sat staring at it with unseeing eyes. *Marital bliss? That's what I'd thought it was, too, but apparently, Randy thought otherwise.*

She glanced around the room, noting the stacks of dirty dishes still waiting to be loaded into the dishwasher, the roaster with the remnants of her famous pepper gravy clinging to its sides, and the pile of silverware she'd set aside to be washed by hand—the silverware she only used for special occasions. As she idly picked up a serving spoon, she had to laugh, despite her feelings of loneliness and despair. *Special occasions? Your husband asking you for a divorce is definitely a special occasion—one in which you never expect to be a participant.*

Placing her flattened palms onto the tabletop for support, she stood with agonizing stiffness, propelled herself one laborious step at a time across the spacious kitchen to the sink, and began to rinse the plates and place them in the dishwasher. Doing it the same way she had done hundreds of times before, but, this time, her mind was far from what she was doing.

Where is Randy this very moment? With that woman?

The question made bile rise in her throat. She picked up one of the delicate crystal goblets Randy had given her on their twentieth anniversary and flung it against the stone fireplace in the corner of the room. The glass shattered, sending shiny shards across the highly polished tile floor. Those glasses had been her prized possession, and she had always washed and dried them by hand to make sure none were ever broken. But today, somehow, the sound of breaking glass felt like a balm poured over her tormented soul.

Is he holding her hand?

A second glass hit the fireplace.

Is he holding Chatalaine in his arms?

The third glass missed its mark and broke against the wall, but she did not care. It was the sound she needed to hear.

Is he kissing that woman?

The fourth and fifth glasses broke simultaneously as she hurled one from each hand toward the fireplace. Sylvia jumped up and down, clapping her hands and laughing hysterically, relieving some of her pent-up tension in this unorthodox manner.

The last two glasses soon joined the others, and they all lay broken on the tile floor, their fragile beauty forever destroyed.

She stood for a long time, mesmerized as she stared at the broken pieces. Somehow, they symbolized the end of her marriage. Her dream. Her life. She wanted to turn and flee from the house she loved. The walls were permeated with memories. Memories she cherished. But today those memories seemed to haunt her, to ridicule her. To tell her she was a fool and a failure. If she had been the wife Randy had wanted, would he have been so easily lured away by that beautiful woman? It was a question she knew she would ask herself time and time again in the weeks to come. *I didn't have a chance*, she reasoned, looking for any excuse to absolve herself and her part in the failure of their marriage. *What woman wouldn't be attracted to Randy? He's not only handsome, he's witty, charming, and highly successful.*

Her thoughts went to Chatalaine and how beautiful she had looked at the restaurant. Her gorgeous blond hair falling softly over her shoulders, her designer suit fitting her like wallpaper, displaying her perfect figure to the fullest advantage, her long slender legs, and fashionable high heels. The striking woman was a walking, talking, real-live Barbie doll.

Finally, willing herself to move, she pulled the dustpan and broom from the pantry, trudged across the kitchen floor, and began to sweep up the mess. Her body became as still as a mannequin when she heard the front door open and close. *Randy?*

"Mom, what happened?"

Disappointed it was not Randy, she turned to face her oldest son, sure that, after what she had been through, she must look like a mess. Even without checking the mirror, she knew her dampened mascara must have left dark streaks down her cheeks, her eyes had to be swollen from crying, and probably her nose was red from rubbing it across her sleeve.

Before she could stop them, two words escaped her lips. "Dad's gone!" She ran to Buck and buried her face in his chest, sudden sobs racking at her body, causing short gasps for air. Everything she had been holding back came gushing forth.

"Gone? What do you mean—*gone?* Is he hurt? Is he at the hospital? Did he have a wreck?" He grabbed onto her arms and pushed her away, staring into her face. "Mom! Tell me! What?"

Sucking in a deep breath, she blurted out, "He—he wants a divorce!"

"What?" Buck began to shake his head. "No, not my dad! He'd never do anything like that. Why are you saying this, Mom? Why?"

"He *is* doing it, Buck. I tried to talk him out of it, but—"

Buck doubled up a fist and plowed it into the palm of his other hand, looking eerily like his father. "It's another woman, isn't it?"

Sylvia nodded as she lowered her head and worked at keeping fresh tears at bay. "He says it isn't."

"That woman at the paper?"

Her eyes widened with surprise. "How did you know she was the one?"

Buck moved to the counter and checked the coffeepot. Finding it empty, he crossed to the cabinet, took out a glass, filled it with water, and took a long, slow drink before setting the empty glass in the sink. "I saw them together," he said, his back still to his mother.

She ran to him and circled her arms around his waist, pressing her face into his strong back. "Oh, Buck, no. You didn't."

He pulled her arms from about him and slowly turned to face her. "It seemed perfectly innocent at the time. I was having lunch with a friend at a little restaurant over in Arlington, and who walks in? Dad, with some woman."

"Did he know you were there?" she asked cautiously, wishing her son had not been forced to become a part of this fiasco.

"Yeah. I waited until they were seated and walked over to them. He introduced her as one of his employees—Catherine, Katrina—something like that. He said they had driven to Arlington to meet with some advertisers, and since it was lunchtime, they decided to have a bite to eat before driving back into Dallas. I believed him then, but now—with Dad talking about divorce, well, I just don't know."

Sylvia covered her face with her hands and tried to control her rekindled rage. "Oh, Buck. Why didn't you tell me? Give me a warning."

He patted her shoulder. "I tried not to give it a second thought. I wanted to believe him and his explanation seemed logical, the way women hold so many managerial positions nowadays."

She examined her heart. "I probably wouldn't have believed you even if you'd brought me back a Polaroid shot of him kissing her. I would've figured out a way to explain it. I trusted him."

"I—I asked Dad later if that was the real reason he was with her."

"You did? What did he say?" Did she really want to hear his answer?

"He really blew up at me. He told me I was a young punk with wild ideas, and he was insulted that I would even consider him being unfaithful to you. I felt like a jerk. He is my dad. The one I've looked up to all my life!"

"He says I should have seen it coming. That I'm to blame in all of this as much as he is." She slipped an arm around her son and hugged him tight. "I guess, if I'd had my eyes open, I should've seen it coming. He's been different for the past few months. Quiet and reserved sometimes, even spacey. Sometimes he was here—yet he wasn't. I should have read the signs. If only I'd—"

"Don't let him do that to you, Mom. Face it. Dad might be a Christian, but he's still a man. A mere mortal. We're all at risk for doing things we know we shouldn't." He gave her a smile that warmed her cold heart and began to melt some of the ice that had begun to form there. "You've been a terrific mom and, from my vantage point, the perfect wife. I can't imagine any woman being able to take your place."

Take my place? Oh, Lord—please—no! She mustered up a smile in return, not wanting him to know how much that phrase upset her. She was grateful for his words of consolation and encouragement, but his last words had pierced her soul. "Thanks, sweetie, but you've seen her. You know how beautiful she is. And young! I can't compete with Chatalaine Vicker."

"Hey, Mom, don't talk that way. You're a real knockout." He gave her chin a playful jab. "Get yourself a bottle of bleach and turn that brown hair of yours into a ditzy blond, take off a few pounds here and there, hit the makeup counters, add a couple of sexy, low-cut dresses and a pair of spike-heeled shoes, and she wouldn't have a chance at taking Dad away from you."

His humor cut through some of the insecurities she was feeling, and she laughed. But her laughter was soon overshadowed by the continual ache in her heart. "I wish I could convince myself it was merely her good looks that drew him to her, but I'm afraid it's much more than that."

Buck frowned, causing deep wrinkles in his forehead. "You—you don't think they're having—"

She reached up and quickly put her hand over his mouth. "Shh, don't even think it."

Buck gently pulled her hand away. "Would you take him back? After the way he's hurt you?"

"Of course, I would," she answered without hesitation. "On our wedding day, I promised before God that I was marrying your father for life, and I meant it. We both said, 'For better and for worse.' God never promised marriage would be easy, Buck."

Buck gave her that shy grin again. "But you had no idea how much worse, *worse* could be or that Dad would do something this bizarre. I'm going to ask Shonna to lock me in the closet if I ever start showing signs of a midlife crisis."

"Buck!" She giggled at his inane comment. "No, I never thought we'd have a problem like this, but I knew I'd have God by my side to help me work out the rough spots. I may have been young, but I wasn't stupid," she added through fresh tears. "I knew what I was vowing. I thought your father did, too."

He grinned a silly little grin. "You do know you look like a raccoon, don't you, Mom?"

She hurried to the little mirror on the back of the pantry door and gazed at her ridiculous reflection, summoning up a smile for his benefit. "I knew I looked bad, but not this bad! Why didn't you tell me?"

"I think you're kinda cute."

She grabbed a dishrag from the drawer, dampened it at the faucet, and began rubbing at the black circles and streaks around her eyes and down her cheeks. "What are you doing here anyway? I thought you and Shonna were spending the rest of the day at her parents' house."

"We are. I left my billfold in the bathroom after that fabulous Thanksgiving dinner you cooked. I came back to get it."

She patted his arm affectionately. "I'm glad you did. I needed someone to talk to. It seems God isn't listening to me."

"Come on, Mom, you know that's not true."

"If He is, why isn't He making your dad come back home where he belongs?"

"Who says He's not trying to convince him to do just that?"

She gestured around the room with a broad sweep of her hand. "Do you see your father here?"

He grabbed it and linked his fingers with hers. "You don't believe God is dealing with Dad? Think about it, Mom. Our father is giving up everything. You know he's got to realize, eventually, he's making a stupid mistake. You have to turn this over to God. Hasn't He promised He'd never leave you or forsake you?"

She pulled her hand free and cradled his chin. "My wonderful, well-grounded son. God does answer prayer. He already has."

He frowned. "What do you mean?"

"He made you leave your billfold in the bathroom, otherwise, why would you have come back here—just when I needed you?"

"See? I told you God answers prayer."

She had to smile at the silly expression on his face. What a joy Buck had been to her since the day he was born. "Yes, He does."

"What now, Mom? Are you going to tell DeeDee and Aaron?"

She crossed the kitchen, seated herself at the table, and began fumbling with the colorful basket of silk flowers she had put together in a craft class at the church. "Not yet. I don't want your brother and sister to know until it's absolutely necessary. And, please, don't tell anyone else about this—except Shonna, of course. I don't want there to be any secrets between the two of you, but ask her to keep this to herself until I'm ready to let everyone know. I want your father to have plenty of time to change his mind. If everyone knows, he'll be embarrassed, and I can't let that happen. Let's give him some time, okay?"

Buck planted a kiss on his mother's cheek. "My faithful, forgiving mother. What a treasure you are. I only hope Dad comes to his senses and realizes it before it's too late."

"Your father needs your prayers, Buck. So do I."

He kissed the tip of her nose. "You got them, both of you."

"Now," she said, trying to put up a brave front and pointing toward the door. "Go to your wife and enjoy what's left of your Thanksgiving Day."

"You gonna be all right? I can stay with you. Shonna will understand."

"I'm going to be fine. I'll call if I need you."

He pulled his cell phone from his belt and held it toward her. "You've got my number?"

She stood on tiptoe and kissed her son's chin. "Yes, I have your number. Go."

As he strode out the door, Sylvia kept the smile on her face, but the minute the door closed behind him, it disappeared, and the feelings of misery and betrayal she had endeavored to squash down deep inside rose to the surface. *Oh, dear God— what a mess we've made of our lives. Only You can straighten this out.*

After sweeping up the broken glass, she took a long, leisurely shower and let the hot water run over her face and body, washing away her tears, until she could stand it no longer. She toweled off and slipped into her pajamas, then dried her hair with the blow dryer and stared into the mirror. Though she fit nicely into a size twelve, her proportions were nothing like Chatalaine's. Giving birth and nursing her children had seen to that. Everything had gone south. She glanced at her reflection and the worn flannel pajamas—the comfortable ones she wore more often than any of her others—and thought about the three delicate, lacy nightgowns she had in her bureau drawer. The ones Randy had bought for her the past three Valentine's Days. Two of them still had the tags on them. The third had only been laundered twice. Why hadn't she worn them? Hadn't Randy told her he had bought them for her because he thought she would look beautiful in them?

Finding it difficult to pray and wondering how God could have let this happen to her, she muttered a few thank-yous, asked God to send Randy home where he belonged, and added a quick, "Amen." Many of the things Randy had mentioned, things that took her away from him, were things she had done at the church. For God. Is this the way He was rewarding her for her labors? By allowing her husband to walk out of her life?

As though God Himself were speaking to her, in her heart she heard, *It wasn't Me that let him go, my child. You turned your back on him and let other things take over your life and become more important than the relationship between the two of you.*

"But, God," she cried out. "Everything I've done has been for a good cause. The church activities. The children. Their school functions. Teaching my Sunday school class. Leading the women's prayer group. Heading up the Care and Share pantry. I did all of those things for You!"

None of it for your own glory? None of it when you should have been with your husband, being a helpmeet to him? When you made those vows before Me, you promised to do many things. Have you honored all of those promises, my daughter?

Sylvia stared at the Bible on her nightstand, remembering their wedding and the way the two of them had placed their hands on a Bible when they had made those vows. "But, Lord,

Randy made those same vows. He's the one who is breaking them, not me! It's not fair that he's expecting me to take part of the blame."

Examine your own heart, daughter. Examine your own heart.

After turning out the light, she lay in the darkness, thinking. Pondering the words God had spoken to her. How many times in the past five years had her husband seemed aloof? Distant. Sometimes acting as if he had no interest in her *or* the children. Had an affair been going on right under her nose, and she had been so absorbed with her life she hadn't noticed? Looking back, the signs had been there. She just had not seen them—or cared enough to see them. The late nights at the office. Sudden trips to the newspaper on weekends to take care of some insignificant problem that cropped up. Calling at the last minute to say he couldn't attend one of the children's school functions. He claimed he was doing those things because of increased competition from both his competitors and the way more people were watching television news to keep them informed rather than the newspapers. Even on the few nights he was home, he would hole up in the den most of the evening and work at the computer. At least, she had *thought* he was working on the computer. Perhaps, instead, he had been talking to Chatalaine on that online Instant Message thing.

Had those excuses been simply that? Excuses to find a way to get out of the house? Away from her? Maybe to meet Chatalaine?

She flipped over onto her side with a groan, her tears flowing again. This would be Randy's first night of staying away from home. Was he having feelings of exhilaration? Or was he, too, feeling pangs of loneliness? She shuddered at how awful it felt being in bed alone. Surely, he was telling her the truth. That nothing was going on between him and that woman. *God, please keep him pure. Don't let him succumb to fleshly desires.*

Without Randy by her side, the bed seemed big. Overpowering. Like an angry giant. She closed her eyes and flattened her hand on his pillow, trying to convince herself that he would be there when she opened them.

He wasn't.

She tugged his pillow to her, drinking in the lingering fragrance of his aftershave and relishing its scent, draping her arm over it much as she did over Randy each night after they turned out the lights. *Oh, Randy. I love you so much. How will I ever live without you? You're my very life!*

four

The last time Sylvia remembered looking at the clock on her nightstand, it was 5:00 a.m. She awakened at eight, feeling like she'd not slept at all, with the sheets askew, and the lovely old nine-patch quilt half off on the floor.

Randy!

She flipped over, her hand quickly moving to his pillow.

But Randy wasn't there.

It hadn't been a bad dream.

He had really left her.

Laboriously, she made the bed, dragging herself from side to side, though why, she didn't know. An unmade bed was the least of her worries. She brushed her teeth and ran a comb through her hair out of habit, not really caring how she looked. Visions of the long-legged blond on the front of the "Dallas Life" section of the newspaper blurred her brain and made her woozy. Her three children had left home. Buck to get married, and Aaron and DeeDee to attend college. Now Randy, her life's mate, was gone, too, and for the first time ever—she was alone. Really alone. Since she and Randy had married so young, she had gone directly from her parents' home to their little apartment, with no stops in-between.

She stood at the window for a long time, gazing into the backyard. With all her busyness, she had even neglected the flowerbeds she had at one time loved. When was the last time she had weeded and fertilized them? Even the perennials had quit blooming. If it weren't for the faithful geraniums, there would be no blooming flowers at all. Thanks to them and their endurance, every few feet a tiny blast of red spotted the otherwise colorless flowerbeds. She winced at the thought. Was her marriage like those flowerbeds? Had she let other things, like the weeds growing so prevalently, go unattended, get in the way, and crowd out the important things of her life until they had withered and died? At the thought, her stomach again turned nauseous, and for a moment, she reeled, clutching the windowsill for support. *Oh, Randy. How could I have taken our life for granted? How could I have taken you for granted? Did I really drive you into that woman's arms?*

Moving slowly into their walk-in closet to pull out her favorite pair of jeans, she froze. Except for a few garments he never wore, Randy's side of the closet was empty. Even the hangers were gone. Shoeboxes no longer filled the long shelves above the rods. No more beautiful designer ties hung from his tie racks. Even the prized rifle his father had given him when he was sixteen no longer stood in the corner behind the clothing where he had kept it so it would be out of sight of the children. Standing on tiptoes, she reached up and ran her hand along the top shelf, in search of the little .25 caliber pistol he always kept there in case an intruder entered their home.

It, too, was gone!

Randy was gone!

Everything was gone!

Her heart thudded to a sudden stop. Surely, he wouldn't do anything foolish! Not her levelheaded Randy!

But the Randy who had told her he was leaving wasn't her levelheaded Randy! He was a stranger wearing Randy's body. She only thought she had known him. This new Randy was an unknown entity, and she had no idea what he might be capable of doing. *Oh, Randy, Randy! If only you would've told me a long time ago how unhappy you were with our marriage, maybe*— She banged her head against the window jamb, but it was too numb even to feel the pain. *If I'd been any kind of attentive wife to you, I should've known. Looking back now, I can see the signs. I'd attributed your silence to you having things on your mind about the paper. All those times when you seemed aloof, I'd thought you were tired. The many times you sat staring at the walls, I assumed you were too physically and mentally exhausted to talk. Were you deliberately ignoring me because you simply no longer wanted to be around me? How could I have been so blind? Why didn't I ask you if something was wrong? Were you seeing Chatalaine even then?*

The image of the elegant woman popped into her mind, uninvited, when she moved toward the bed, pausing at the full-length mirror on the way. Her breath caught and nearly gagged her as she stared at her reflection. *Can this be me? Where is that young woman my husband used to admire? The one whose hair was brown and shiny, instead of dull and graying? The one who was twenty pounds lighter and cared about her figure? Who always put her makeup on first thing in the morning and went out of her way to kiss her husband good-bye when he left for work? The one who hung on his every word, making sure she was there whenever he needed her?* She glanced down at her faded jeans and the well-worn T-shirt that had become the *uniform* she crawled into when she came home from one of her functions, eager to make herself comfortable. *When did I decide it was no longer necessary to look my best at the end of the day when Randy came home from work? When did I become so careless?*

Grabbing her robe from the chair where she had left it, she draped it over the mirror, shutting out the image that threatened to destroy what little self-esteem she had left. But it didn't help. The reflection remained etched on her memory, and she did not like the feeling.

She had to talk to Randy. To beg him to come back home where he belonged.

"Good morning. *Dallas Times*. If you know your party's extension, you may enter it now, otherwise listen to the complete list of options before making your selection," the canned recording said when she dialed the phone. She punched in the numbers by rote and waited for him to answer.

"Good morning. Randy Benson's office. This is Carol. May I ask who's calling?"

Instantly, Sylvia realized she had dialed the extension for Randy's office and not his direct line. "Ah—Carol—this is Sylvia. May I speak to Randy?"

"I'm sorry, Sylvia. He isn't in. He's in meetings over in Arlington most of the day. I don't expect him back until late this afternoon."

A meeting in Arlington or another one of his rendezvous?

"When he's out of the office, he usually checks in with me several times a day. Would you like me to have him phone home?"

"Yes, would you, please? I'll—I'll be here all day. I really need to talk to him."

"Would you like me to try and reach him?"

"No, just tell him when you hear from him." She thanked the woman, then hit the OFF button, and placed the phone back onto the charger, disappointed.

She had no more than lifted her hand from it, when it rang. She snatched it up, both hoping it was Randy, yet not sure what she would say if he did call. "Hello."

"Hi, Mom. I've been concerned about you. Are you okay? Do you want me to come over?"

As much as she loved hearing her oldest son's voice, she was filled with disappointment. "No, honey, I'm—I'm okay. Just depressed."

"I love you, Mom. You know I'll come if you need me."

She smiled into the phone. At least her son still loved her. "No, I don't want you taking off work. Don't worry about me, sweetie. I'm still hoping, praying, somehow this will all work out."

"I still want to call Dad."

"I know, but please don't. Let's make it as easy as possible for your father to come back home, and I don't want there to be any rifts between the two of you."

"Okay, but if you—"

"I know, and thanks, Buck. Get back to your job. Your mother will survive."

"Survive?" she repeated aloud when she hung up the phone. "I'm not so sure I *will* survive or even want to if Randy doesn't come back home."

She busied herself doing several loads of laundry, weeping when she pulled a couple of Randy's favorite shirts from the hamper. Her tears fell softly onto the fabric when she cradled them close, the faint aroma of his aftershave tantalizing her nostrils. When the last piece had been pulled from the dryer and folded, she closed the laundry room door and made her way into the kitchen, checking the clock as she moved to the refrigerator and pulled out a bottle of cranberry juice. It was nearly noon, and she hadn't eaten a bite of breakfast or even had a glass of water.

Why hasn't he called? Surely, Carol has heard from him by now.

She jumped for the phone when it rang about three, but it was not Randy calling; it was Buck, checking on her again.

An hour later, a telemarketer called, offering to give her an estimate on siding. Normally, she listened courteously to their spiel before saying, "No, thank you," and hanging up, but not this time. This time his call infuriated her, and she cut him off right after his "Are you the homeowner?" question.

For the next hour, she sat staring at the phone.

But it didn't ring.

Nor did it ring at six, or seven, eight, nine, ten, or eleven, other than two more calls from Buck.

When the doorbell rang at half past eight the next morning, she rushed to answer it, stubbing her toe on the ottoman on the way, but it was the UPS man bringing a package. Something Randy had ordered from a computer supply company.

Other than Buck's regular concerned calls, the phone did not ring a single time on Saturday, and Sylvia found herself in a deep pit of depression with the walls closing in on her. Why didn't Randy call? If only he had left the phone number where he would be staying. She was tempted to look up Chatalaine Vicker's number in the phonebook but decided against it. Whether Randy was at her place or not, he would be furious with her for checking up on him. She tried watching TV to keep her mind off him, but that didn't work. Next, she pulled out the quilt she had started when their children were small and had never finished. Maybe the rhythm of working the needle would help sooth her jagged nerves, but she found she had misplaced her thimble, so she returned it to its box in the family room closet. The novel in her bedside chest held no more interest than it had a day or two before and ended up back in the drawer.

In desperation, she turned to her Bible for solace, but even it did not help. A bookmark fell out onto the bed as she closed its cover. Her gaze locked on the quotation printed there in a beautiful script. Its message ripped her heart to shreds. *Love thrives in the face of all life's hazards, except one. Neglect.* The words ricocheted through her being, replaying over and over, bathing her heart with guilt. She *had* neglected Randy! *Oh, dear Lord, what have I done? Help me, I pray! Help me put our marriage back together!*

At seven the next morning, after another sleepless night, she phoned Jen, her pastor's wife and best friend. "I won't be able to teach my class today," she told her, trying to make her voice sound raspy, as if she were coming down with something. She knew if she ran into any of her friends, her face would immediately tell them she had a problem without a word being spoken. Her swollen eyes and reddened cheeks, too, would be a dead giveaway, even if she could keep her tears in check, which she knew would be impossible.

"I'm sure Randy is taking good care of you, Sylvia, but if there's anything I can do—" Jen laughed. "Like open a can of chicken noodle soup, heat it in my microwave, and bring it over to you, I'd—"

"I know," Sylvia answered, interrupting, but the last thing she needed was to have to explain her appearance to someone. "There's really nothing you can do, but thanks, I appreciate the offer. I—I think I'll just rest and take it easy."

She stayed in her pajamas and robe all morning, mostly just sitting in Randy's recliner, rubbing her hands over the armrests, and staring out the pair of sliding glass doors, watching the birds feed at the birdfeeder he'd built for her for Mother's Day four or five years ago. She had spent many happy hours watching the cardinals and blue jays sort through the seeds, picking out the kinds they liked best.

Buck stopped by about one o'clock, bringing her cartons of sweet and sour chicken, fried rice, and crab Rangoon from her favorite Chinese restaurant. Although she appreciated his efforts and concern and thanked him with an enthusiasm she did not feel, the food was tasteless and held no appeal. He took out the trash before leaving, telling her he'd be back the next day, but to call if she needed anything in the meantime. He explained Shonna had wanted to come with him, but he'd told her it might be best if she waited until Sylvia was feeling up to seeing her. She thanked him, saying she would phone Shonna in a day or two. Maybe then she would feel more like talking about things.

After sleeping most of the afternoon, she ate a bit more of the rice about seven and crawled into bed at eight, facing another sleepless night without her husband by her side.

She phoned Randy's office again on Monday, this time punching in the numbers to his direct line. It rang four times before Carol picked up in the outer office.

"I'm sorry, Sylvia. He is in a staff meeting. I am afraid it is going to be a lengthy one. He has already asked me to call the deli and have box lunches delivered. But I'll tell him you called."

Sylvia let her head drop to her chest with an, "Oh. Of course. I forgot. He always has staff meetings on Monday."

Seeming to sense a problem, Carol offered, "If it's important, maybe I can interrupt."

"No! Don't do that. Just ask him to call, please."

She stayed by the phone the rest of the day, watching the hours tick by, waiting for his call.

But it never came.

When the phone rang Tuesday morning, she grabbed it up on the first ring.

"Mrs. Benson. This is Hank from Hawkins Flowers. Could you please tell Mr. Benson we were able to get the apricot roses after all? He seemed so disappointed when he ordered and had to settle for pink roses. I knew he'd want to know."

"Apricot roses?"

"Yes, and tell him we delivered them with his note attached, just as he'd asked. My driver said the lady was thrilled with them. Whoops, the other line is ringing. Thank you for conveying my message. Mr. Benson is a good customer, and we appreciate his business."

Sylvia stood with her mouth hanging open as the broken connection clicked in her ear. When the man had called, she had hoped the flowers were for her, and her heart had soared. Then he had said they had already been delivered. To whom had he sent flowers? Certainly not her! There seemed to be only one answer.

Chatalaine.

Why else would he go to all the trouble to make sure he was able to get roses of a certain color?

She staggered her way across the family room and plunked herself into Randy's recliner. When was the last time he had sent flowers to her? Her birthday? No, he had taken the whole family out to celebrate, but there had been no flowers for her. Usually, he sent her a gigantic poinsettia for Christmas, but this past year, he did not even do that. Mother's Day last year? No, Buck and his wife had given her a beautiful white orchid corsage, but Randy had barely told her, "Happy Mother's Day." She cupped her head in her hands, her fingers rubbing at her eyes wearily as the song "You Don't Bring Me Flowers Anymore" resonated through her head. No, her beloved husband did not bring her flowers anymore. Apparently, his flowers were going to someone else now. Someone who paid more attention to him and met his needs more adequately than she did.

As Sylvia lay in bed that night, she came to a decision. If Randy would not return her calls, she would go see him at his office. Yes, that is exactly what she would do.

By nine the next morning, her hair swept up in a twist, her makeup meticulously applied, and decked out in the dress she'd bought on impulse several weeks earlier, Sylvia was in the elevator on her way up to Randy's fourth-floor office. She had decided it was a bit too tight for her and a bit too short and had almost returned it to the store. Now she was glad she hadn't. She had purposely worn the necklace and matching earrings he had given her several Christmases ago, although she doubted he would remember. Normally, she wore shoes with less than two-inch heels, but this morning she was wearing the pair of strappy, spike-heeled sandals she'd purchased to wear to one of Randy's award banquets. She had ended up not going and staying home because DeeDee complained of a sore throat. She had never worn the shoes long enough to break them in, and her feet were killing her. However, if it meant catching her husband's attention, the pain would be worth it.

"My, you look nice," Carol said as Sylvia exited the elevator, "but I'm sorry. You just missed him. He hasn't been gone five minutes."

Sylvia wanted to cry. And nearly did. But knowing her tears would only upset Carol, she reined them in and forced a casual smile. "He didn't know I was coming. I thought I'd surprise him." Her heart broken and tears threatening to erupt despite her tight hold on them, she said a quick good-bye to Carol and stepped back into the waiting elevator. She had so hoped to see Randy and talk to him. Maybe then she could convince him to swallow his pride and admit he wanted to come home.

She exited the elevator and hurried out the front door toward the *Dallas Times's* public parking garage to the left of the big building. But as she approached the entrance, a white minivan exited through the gate not thirty feet in front of her, her husband at the wheel and a gorgeous blond in the passenger seat.

Devastated by the sight, Sylvia leaned against the building for support, both hurt and angry. *He doesn't have time to return my calls, but he sure has time for his little cutie!* Lifting first one foot, then the other, she snatched off the offensive sandals from her aching feet and ran the rest of the way to her car in her stockings, not caring if anyone saw her or if she got runs in her new pantyhose. All she wanted to do was get home where she could hide out and unleash her overwhelming rage. *How dare he?*

Finally, she reached the house, not even sure which route she had taken. She flung herself across the bed and screamed out to God, asking what she had done in her life that was so bad she would deserve this kind of treatment.

When the doorbell sounded at four, she couldn't decide if she should answer it or not. It might be Randy, and at this point, she was not sure she even wanted to talk to him. If she told him she had seen him with Chatalaine, he would probably make up some ridiculous excuse. Or maybe he would just admit it, and she wasn't sure she was ready to hear those words from his lips.

The doorbell rang a second time. She stood pressed against the wall, weighing her options.

Whoever was there began pounding on the door. Since she had not changed the locks, she knew if it were Randy, he would just use his key. So rather than explain to whomever might be there, she opened the door.

"I knew you were here. Your car is in the driveway, and your keys are hanging in the front door. You'd better be more careful."

five

"Jen!" Sylvia quickly wiped at her eyes with her sleeve. "I—I didn't know it was you!"

Jen moved inside and stood glaring at her, her face filled with concern. "Aw, sweetie, what's wrong? You look awful!"

Sylvia turned and led the way into the living room. "I–I'd rather not talk about it."

Jen took her hand and tugged her toward the flowery chintz sofa. "Look, Sylvia, you're my best friend. If you think I'm going to walk out that door before I find out what's bothering you, you're crazy. Now, sit down here beside me and tell me about it, or I'm going to call Randy's office and ask him." Giving her a quick once-over, she continued. "You're all dressed up. Were you on your way out?" Spotting her stocking'd feet, she raised her brows and gave her a smile. "You forgot your shoes."

Sylvia leaned back against the sofa's soft cushions and closed her eyes. She needed to talk to someone. She hated to confide in Buck. After all, Randy was his dad, but she had to open up her injured heart to someone. The silence was driving her wild.

"Okay, out with it. What's wrong? You know you can trust me, don't you?" Jen placed her hand softly on Sylvia's arm. "You're doubly safe talking to me. As your best friend, I'd never betray your confidence, and as the wife of your pastor, I'm bound by God to keep my mouth shut."

Sylvia opened her eyes and stared at the ceiling. "I don't know who I can trust, Jen."

"Out with it, Sylvia. It'll make you feel better to talk about it. Are you sick? Has one of the kids gotten into trouble?"

"Worse than that."

Jen paused. "How much worse?"

Sylvia turned to her friend. She could be trusted, and she would never do or say anything that would harm either her or Randy. "Randy—he—"

Jen let out a gasp. "Oh, no! Is there something wrong with Randy? Harrison and I were just saying the other day, that man is the picture of health."

"No, he's fine. Healthwise."

Jen looked at her impatiently. "Then what about Randy?"

"He wants a di–divorce."

Her friend just stared at her in disbelief, as if words failed her. Finally, she slipped her arm about Sylvia and pulled her close. "I'm so sorry, Sylvia."

Sylvia gulped hard, then for the next half hour, she related the entire story about Randy's leaving and her suspicion he'd left her for another woman, even though he'd denied it. She was careful not to mention Chatalaine's name. "I'm at my wit's end. I've about decided to give up and let him have the divorce without contesting it."

When she finished, Jen asked, "You, Sylvia Benson, are going to give up? Without a fight? That is not like you. If you still love this man and want him back, you are going to have to slug it out for him. This pity party you're having isn't going to cut it. It only makes you look weak, and from my vantage point as a pastor's wife with experience in dealing with broken marriages, weak is never appealing or convincing to the spouse who walked out on the marriage. Especially if there is another woman involved. She's usually pulling out all the stops to get the man to leave his wife and marry her. It's her mission in life, her goal, and she won't quit until she gets him."

Sylvia looked at her with wide eyes, surprised by Jen's direct words. "If that's true, how do you expect me to compete?"

"That, friend of mine, is for you to figure out! But if it were me, and I loved my husband as much as I thought you loved Randy, I'd fight for him with every ounce of my being."

Sylvia pulled away from her and lowered herself into Randy's recliner. "I wouldn't begin to know how to fight. She—she's—" She selected her words carefully, even though she knew, as a pastor's wife, her friend would never go about telling tales and break a confidence. "She's beautiful, Jen."

Jen did a double take. "You've seen her?"

Sylvia nodded. "It's that society columnist from Randy's paper."

"Chatalaine Vicker?"

"Yes."

"Wow. You are right. She is beautiful!"

"Now you see why I said I couldn't compete with her."

Jen shook her head sadly. "I always thought, as happily married as the two of you seemed, Randy would be the last man to succumb to infidelity, but no man is safe. Or woman, for that matter. Many women leave their husbands and kids for so-called *greener pastures,* only to find they weren't as green as they'd expected." Jen seated herself on the sofa and leaned back into the cushions. "He sure wouldn't be the first Christian man his age to let his head be turned by a pretty woman. Is he wearing gold chains, leaving his top three buttons unbuttoned on his shirt so his chest hair will show, and talking about buying a motorcycle?"

Sylvia smiled through her tears. "Not that I've seen."

"Then there may be hope for him."

"You think he may be going through a midlife crisis?"

Jen shrugged. "Who knows? We women have menopause— men have a midlife crisis. We get grouchy. They get childish. All of a sudden, they need their space. We've seen it over and over again during our years in the ministry. I can't begin to tell you how many times my husband has had to counsel couples in this very situation. Usually, if both partners love the Lord, the husband comes to his senses before anything stupid happens, and if each person wants to revive the marriage and is willing to compromise and do their part, their relationship can be salvaged."

Sylvia sniffled as she reached for a tissue. "Salvaged? You make it sound like a battleship that went down at sea, was found, and pulled up later—battered and covered with barnacles."

"In some ways, that's what a broken marriage is like. But unlike the battleship, it sinks slowly—with the husband and wife barely noticing the leak that will eventually destroy it. Funny, you mentioned barnacles. I've heard my husband use those very words when he's been counseling a couple. He often likens them to wounds that married folks inflict on each other over time—like hastily said words, forgetting birthdays and anniversaries, neglecting to say I love you, taking each other for granted, not spending time together, and on and on and on."

Jen reached across and squeezed her hand. "The wounds are tiny at first, barely noticeable, but then infection sets in, and the wounds fester and grow until they actually threaten life if left unattended. Placing a Band-Aid over them merely covers them, but underneath the wounds remain infected, spreading wider and wider until they demand attention. At that point, drastic measures have to be taken. Though the wounds can probably be treated successfully with time and attention, many folks prefer immediate surgery. Cut it off and get rid of it."

"Divorce."

Jen nodded. "Yes, divorce. Sometimes those hurts go way deeper than we can possibly imagine."

The two women sat silently staring at one another. Finally, Sylvia spoke. "I—I've neglected Randy, Jen. I've put everything ahead of him and his needs. I realize that now."

"I'm afraid, as women and mothers, we all have a tendency to do that very thing. And for worthwhile causes. But that doesn't make it right." Jen confessed. "I have to admit, sometimes I feel neglected. Being married to a pastor doesn't mean everything is hunky-dory at all times. We get calls all hours of the day and night from people who need him. I've cooked many a supper only to have him call and say he won't make it home because someone is having trouble and needs him. As the pastor's family, the children and I always take the backseat in any situation. Harrison and I have our moments of conflict, too. We have the same pressures and problems our church members have; only we're expected to be perfect. The power of darkness would like nothing more than to see trouble in the pastor's home, and the enemy works twenty-four/seven to make it happen."

Sylvia stared at her friend. "You and Harrison? But—you two are perfect. I've never once heard you say a cross word to each other!"

"That's because we keep our best face forward and do our arguing within the four walls of our home." Jen leaned forward, bracing her hands on her knees, her face serious. "Look, Sylvia, no one is perfect. Not you. Not Randy. Not Harrison and certainly not me. Marriages are fragile things. We can't let them go unattended or take them for granted. I know Harrison and I have to work at it constantly. Several years ago, we realized, due to the demands of life, we were drifting apart and decided to do something about it. That's why Friday night is our night. Unless an emergency happens, which it does quite often, from five o'clock until midnight every Friday night, the two of us are together. Alone. No kids. No in-laws. No parishioners. Just my husband and me. One week I plan the evening. The next week, Harrison plans it. It's always a surprise. It may be as simple as hamburgers at McDonald's and a movie or a picnic in the park.

Other times it's as complex as a dinner theater. But it's our time together. We've even sneaked out of town a few times and spent the night at a motel." Jen's eyes sparkled as she talked.

"I wish Randy and I had done something like that." Sylvia leaned back in Randy's recliner and stared at the ceiling, trying to remember the last time she and her husband had spent the entire evening together, just the two of them. "Maybe if we had, he'd still be here."

"Men try to act real tough, put on a façade. Rarely do they admit they're hurting. They pretend they have tough skin, but they're as vulnerable as we are, honey. If someone had asked me which man in our church would be least likely to do something like this, I would have said Harrison first, with Randy running a very close second."

Sylvia blinked back tears. "Me, too. I never dreamed—"

"That's the problem, Sylvia. Most of us don't even suspect a problem until it rears its ugly head. We're too caught up with life to see what's right under our nose."

"Do—do you think it's too late to fix it?"

"Let me ask *you* a question. Do you think God wants the two of you together?"

Without hesitation, Sylvia answered, "Yes! Of course, He does."

"Then fight, Sylvia! Fight with all you're worth. If you must go down, go down swinging."

"Fight?"

Jen doubled up her fist and punched at the air. "Yes, fight. Fight for your marriage."

Sylvia let out a sigh. "But I'm not a fighter. I wouldn't know how to begin."

"You? Not a fighter? I've always thought of you as a fighter. Aren't you the woman who went to bat with the city council over the zoning for the church's youth building annex and won? I was amazed the day you spoke at that council meeting. I never knew you had it in you. You were so passionate and articulate, they had no choice but to grant the zoning to you. I can't think of anyone who could have done a better job."

Sylvia smiled a small victorious smile. "I really wanted the youth of our church to have that annex."

"And you did all you could to make it happen, didn't you? You moved way out of your comfort zone. You have to do the same thing now if you want to win." Jen scooted to the edge of the sofa. "If you want to revive this marriage, you're going to have to face up to your part in its failure and do something about it."

"Like what? What can I do?"

"That question, my friend, is one you'll have to answer." Jen pulled her car keys from her pocket and rose to her feet. "I hate to leave you like this, but I have to pick up one of the children, and I'm already late. I will give you this bit of advice, though. Like you, I'm sure God wants the two of you together, so why don't you let Him help you with the answer? Pray about it, Sylvia. Listen to God. Read His Word. If your heart is open and you're willing to do whatever He asks, He'll tell you how."

Sylvia pushed herself out of the recliner and stood, her heart overflowing with love and appreciation for this godly woman. "I'm glad you came, Jen."

"Me, too, even though I had to pound on the door to get you to let me in." Jen gave her arm an affectionate pinch. "I'll be praying for you, you know that."

"I'm counting on it."

Sylvia stood in the doorway, waving at her friend and confidante as she drove off. God had sent her at just the right time. With renewed hope in her heart, she closed the door.

Reading her Bible that night, Jen's words kept coming back to her. *If you want to revive this marriage, you are going to have to face up to your part in its failure and do something about it.*

"But what, Lord? What can I do?" Sylvia cried out after she dropped to her knees beside her bed. "I've left messages nearly every day, and Randy hasn't returned any of my calls. I've gone to his office only to find he left with that woman. I don't know what to do. Jen says I have to fight for him, but how? How do I fight? Show me what to do. Surely, you want Randy and me together. Help me, God! Give me wisdom. Give me guidance!"

No flash appeared.

No revelation from heaven.

As she lay there in the darkened room, Sylvia continued to pray, quoting every scripture verse she had memorized about God answering prayer. Eventually, she fell asleep, the pillow wet with her tears.

⋅⋅⋅

It was after midnight when Randy crawled into bed in his new fifth-floor, high-rise apartment. Why hadn't he noticed the noise from the nearby set of elevators when he had leased it? And who could be going up and down in it this time of night, anyway? How did they expect a guy to sleep with all that racket?

He flipped onto his side and pulled the sheet over his head. Morning would arrive soon enough, and he needed to be at the office early to prepare for a meeting with one of his key advertisers. Unable to fall asleep, he ran the meeting's agenda over in his head, hoping to come up with a few more reasons why the client should up his advertising budget for the coming year. Circulation was down as more and more people turned to CNN for their daily news. And with the cost of production going up every day, it was becoming harder and harder to meet the anticipated yearly profit margin. Maybe he should have gone with CNN when they had given him the chance. They'd made him a good offer, but that would have meant moving to Atlanta.

Though he'd known she really didn't want to, Sylvia had even said she was willing to make the move.

Sylvia! Why did his thoughts on any subject seem to end up with Sylvia, when he had finally gotten up the courage to move out of the house and put an end to their stagnant marriage? Now that he was going to be free to do whatever he chose, maybe he should contact CNN again and see if they were still interested in his joining their staff. The kids were grown. He could always hop on a plane and come back to visit them whenever he wanted, and he could send them tickets to come and visit him. Atlanta was an exciting city, with lots of things to see and do. Sylvia would love the Antebellum Plantation and shopping at the trendy Lenox Square Mall.

Sylvia! There I go again!

He kicked off the covers and rolled onto his back, staring at the tiny slivers of light creeping in around the edges of the Venetian blind. *I wonder how she's doing? I guess it was pretty lousy of me to tell her I wanted a divorce on Thanksgiving Day, but I've tried several times to tell her, and there never seemed to be a right time. She'll get used to me being gone. No more picking up after me, doing my laundry, cooking my meals.*

His thoughts went to the pile of dirty shirts, underwear, and socks piled up on the chair. He would have to take care of them this weekend. The apartment manager had told him there was a coin-operated laundry room on the basement level. Maybe he would just wash them himself. How hard could it be? Toss them in, add the soap, and pop in a few quarters. In all the years they had been married, he had never once done a single load of laundry. Sylvia had always done it. His clean clothes were always either hung in his closet or folded neatly in his bureau. He had never even taken his suits to the cleaners. She had done that, too. Had he ever thanked her? Surely, he had. No, come to think of it, he hadn't. Doing laundry had been part of her job, just as getting to the newspaper office by seven had been his. Had *she* ever thanked him for bringing home *his* paycheck?

As he lay there, other things Sylvia had done over the years played out in his mind. The house had always been clean, with things put in their proper places even though, at times, she'd had a sick child to tend to or felt ill herself, but she'd done them without complaining or asking for credit. The meals appeared on the table as if by magic. He'd never given a second thought to when she'd had time to do the shopping. Not once had he stopped to calculate the time she'd spend in the kitchen peeling vegetables, browning meat, preparing casseroles, baking pies and cakes, or trying out new recipes she thought he'd enjoy.

She had become quite handy around the house at doing repairs, too. She'd even asked for a cordless drill and screwdriver for Christmas a few years ago so she could put a decorative molding up in their bedroom and a chair rail on the dining room wall. At the time, he had laughed, then humored her by buying them for her. Why hadn't he put those things up for her himself? Didn't she have enough to do? Well, he was busy, too. Working ten-hour days took its toll on a man. *Come on, Randy, be honest with yourself. You could have done those things for her, but you'd rather play racquetball with a client or watch a football game on TV. You weren't exactly a model husband.*

He rammed a fist into the empty pillow beside him, then flipped over onto his stomach. *Enough! I've got to get some Zs! I've made my decision, and there's no turning back. I waited way too long as it is. It's my time now, and Sylvia is just going to have to learn to live with it!*

≈

The ringing of the phone brought Sylvia out of a fitful sleep.

six

She dove to answer it, hoping it was Randy.

"Good morning, Betty," the voice on the other end said cheerily. "This is your wake-up call."

Quickly sitting up on the side of the bed, Sylvia stared at the red numbers on the clock. Five a.m. "What? Who did you want? Betty? There's no Betty here."

"Whoops, sorry," a male voice said apologetically. "I must've dialed the wrong number. I promised my girlfriend I'd call at five. She has a plane to catch at seven. I hope I didn't wake you."

"It's okay," she mumbled before dropping the phone back into its cradle. After blinking several times, she stared at the clock, then lay back on the bed, snuggling under the covers and into the twisted nest of sheets and blankets she'd created by her night of tossing and turning.

"Okay, God. It's You and me here, and I need help. What can I do? I need a plan." As she lay there, praying and waiting on the Lord, she began to, once again, go over the scripture verses she had learned as a child and in her adult Sunday school classes. At one time, she had even enrolled in the Navigator's Scripture Memory Course.

"All things work together for good to them that love God. . . ."

"Trust in the Lord with all thine heart; and lean not unto thine own understanding. . . .

"Now abideth faith, hope, charity, these three; but the greatest of these is charity. . . ."

"Who can find a virtuous woman? for her price is far above rubies. The heart of her husband doth safely trust in her, so that he

shall have no need of spoil. . . ."

"Spoil," she said aloud. "Could that mean another woman? Umm, let me see. What else does the thirty-first chapter of Proverbs have to say about the perfect marriage?"

"She will do him good and not evil all the days of her life."

"Haven't I done that for Randy?"

Delving into the recesses of her memory, she continued into the chapter and quoted each scripture as she'd learned it from the King James Version of the Bible.

"Her children arise up, and call her blessed; her husband also, and he praiseth her. Many daughters have done virtuously, but thou excellest them all."

Not me, Father God. I put everyone else's needs above those of my husband.

"Favour is deceitful, and beauty is vain: but a woman that feareth the Lord, she shall be praised. Give her of the fruit of her hands; and let her own works praise her in the gates."

She tried to go on to other scriptures she had learned, but the last verse of Proverbs thirty-one kept ringing in her heart, and she began to repeat it over and over. *"Give her of the fruit of her hands; and let her own works praise her in the gates. Give her of the fruit of her hands; and let her own works praise her in the gates."* "What are you trying to tell me, Lord? What am I missing here?"

"Give her of the fruit of her hands; and let her own works praise her in the gates." Why was He impressing this verse upon her?

Suddenly, it came to her. The plan she needed. Of course! It was perfect. She and Randy needed to go back to where they started. Learn to love each other all over again. Learn to appreciate one another and what they had each contributed to their marriage! Let their own works praise them in the gates!

ক

Randy sat behind his big desk and stared at the business plan he had spent hours preparing for his key client. Well, things happened. It wasn't the man's fault his wife had to be rushed to the hospital with a drop in her sodium levels. He glanced at the open book on his desk. His next appointment wasn't until one o'clock, which gave him time to work on several other pressing things he had put aside in order to work on the business plan.

"Mr. Benson." His name crackled over the intercom on his desk.

"Yes, Carol, what is it?"

"Your wife is here."

Randy frowned at the intercom. Sylvia was in the outer office? He had refrained from returning her calls, unable to face the crying scene he knew would come if he talked to her. "Ah—" he said slowly, trying to think quickly of an excuse to turn her away.

"I told her your nine o'clock appointment cancelled."

Carol! You shouldn't have done that. Now I don't have an excuse for not seeing her. "I'll—I'll be right out." *Maybe she won't cause a scene if I talk to her in the outer office,* he reasoned as he rose and headed toward the door.

He was not prepared for the sight that greeted him.

❧

Sylvia tugged at her skirt, then smoothed her jacket. *Why didn't I wear the taupe pantyhose instead of this black pair? I wonder if my hair looks okay? Should I have put on more lipstick? Is the neckline on this blouse too low cut? Why didn't I check myself out in the mirror in the ladies' room before coming up here? Oh, my, I'm a nervous wreck!*

Her heart was pounding way beyond the speed limit as the door to her husband's office opened and he stepped out, dressed in his black Armani suit, starched white shirt, and the black and white polka dot tie she had given him for Christmas. He badly needed a haircut, making the long silver streaks combed back from his temples even more attractive. "Hi, Randy," she said, conjuring up the sweetest voice and smile possible and holding up a white bag with the words *Moon Doggie's Bakery* emblazoned on it in big red letters. "I hope you've got time for a coffee break. I've brought your favorites. Chocolate Éclairs from Moon Doggie's!"

"Well, lucky you," Carol told her boss with a smile, "to have such a thoughtful wife."

Right away, Sylvia knew Randy hadn't told anyone at the office about their breakup, unless he had told Chatalaine. Without waiting for him to invite her in, she brushed past him and into his office, going to the little counter where Carol kept his coffeepot turned on all day. "Sit down," she said, grinning at him. "I'll put these on one of your paper plates and pour us each a cup of coffee." She could feel Randy's eyes boring into her.

"What are you doing, Syl?"

She turned slowly and gave him a coquettish grin and a tilt of her head. "Pouring my husband a cup of coffee."

"You know what I mean. Why are you here?"

Placing their cups on the desk, she scurried back to the counter for their plates and napkins. "Can't a wife surprise her husband once in a while?"

"Don't you think that it's a bit late for games? We are not teenagers."

His retort was cool, but she ignored it and continued to smile as she pulled a chair up close to the desk and settled herself into it. Her feet were killing her in the spike heels, but she kept smiling anyway, ignoring the pain. "Napkin?" she asked, reaching one out to him.

"I don't get it." He took a swig of coffee after blowing into his cup, and all the while, he stared at her. "I've never seen you like this. You're so—dressed up—for nine o'clock in the morning. Is that a new dress?"

Yes, it's a new dress. I bought it several weeks ago, because I knew it was your favorite color, to wear to the awards banquet you wanted me to attend with you. But instead, I ended up going to the hospital with old Mrs. Taylor when she had her heart attack, and you went on alone. "It's pretty new. I haven't had it very long." She stood and, smiling, did a pirouette. "You like it?"

His eyes widened, and he continued to stare at her. "Yeah, I like it. As a matter of fact, you look terrific."

Good, that's what I wanted you to think. Otherwise, I wouldn't have worn these ridiculous shoes. "It's a bit more youthful than I usually wear, but hey, I'm still young!" she said, adding a merry chuckle. "I have years ahead of me."

"We both do." His tone seemed a bit melancholy to her, or was she imagining it and hoping he was as miserable without her as she was without him?

"I'd like for us to spend those years together, Randy."

He cleared his throat loudly, then rose from his chair. "My mind is made up, Syl. If you've come here thinking you'll change it with a bag of éclairs, you're wrong."

"Sit down, Randy, please. I haven't come here to make a scene. I'm not planning on having a shouting session, unless that's what you want. Your news hit me hard, I'll admit that, but I now realize many of your reasons for wanting to end our marriage were valid. Neither of us has been doing our part to make this relationship succeed." *But at least I don't have a boyfriend waiting in the wings!*

He slumped back in his chair with a look of defeat. "So what do you want, Syl? I told you I still planned to take care of you and the kids."

"I'm not concerned about that, Randy." She reached across the desk and covered his hand with hers, relieved when he made no attempt to pull it away. "I—I love you. I always have.

I always will, even if you go through with the divorce."

"I've already talked to my attorney, Syl. He's drawing up the papers."

"Randy, I've thought over the things you said, and looking back, although my heart was in the right place, my body wasn't. I should have been there for you. Instead, I've put the needs of others, the children, and the church ahead of you and your needs. But you were always so self-sufficient and didn't seem to need me. I just assumed you didn't mind when you had to go places and do things alone. You never complained. Not really. And *you* served on the church board. That took you away many evenings while I sat at home alone. Was that so different from what I was doing? We both accepted Jesus as our Savior, and we both love the Lord and want to serve Him—sometimes His work takes us away when we'd like to spend the evening at home."

"I'm going to resign from the church board, Syl," he admitted in an almost whisper. "When the word gets out we're getting a divorce, I doubt Harrison or any of the members of the church will want me serving as their deacon."

Especially not if you're leaving me for another woman! It hurt her that he avoided her gaze.

"I—I haven't told anyone here at the office or at the church yet—about us, but I suppose you've told Jen, since she is your best friend."

She wanted to lie, but she couldn't, not if she expected him to be truthful with her. "Yes, I told her, but I'm sure it will go no further than Harrison."

"You're probably right. They're good people."

"People who have the same problems as anyone else."

He nodded as he fidgeted with the handle on his cup. "I guess. They're human, too."

"I've come here today, Randy, prepared to make you a deal."

He raised his head and stared wide-eyed at her. "Short of saying *yes* to a divorce, I don't know what kind of a deal you can offer."

"Like I said, I still love you and don't want our marriage to end. So—here is the deal. I'll give you your divorce, uncontested, if you'll do one thing for me."

The look of relief in his eyes nearly made her cry. "What?"

"I want us to have one last Christmas together."

He shook his head slowly. "You mean you want me to move back in until after Christmas? No way! Leaving this time was hard enough. I'll not do it a second time!" He rose and moved around the desk toward the door.

"Your call, Randy. Do you want me to make a scene here in your office?"

He turned back to her. "Of course not!"

"Then sit down and listen to me."

৵

Randy did as he was told and settled back into his chair, staring at his wife of twenty-five years. He had never seen her like this, and her demeanor confused him. This wasn't the Sylvia he knew, the one who always walked away from him rather than have a confrontation, the woman who could never refuse anyone who asked for help.

And what was she doing dressed like this? She rarely wore short skirts that revealed her knees. And she was right. It was much more youthful than she usually wore, but in all the right places. She looked like she had just stepped out of the beauty shop. Every hair was perfect. Her makeup, which she rarely wore, made her skin look—oh, he couldn't think of a word to describe it, but she looked good. Really good.

"Before we shut the door on our marriage and we each go our separate ways, I want us to spend the week of Christmas together."

"Impossible. Christmas is a busy time here at the—"

"You haven't taken a day's vacation yet this year, Randy, and I know you have at least three weeks coming. Surely, if you want a divorce as badly as you say you do, you can manage a week off." She stood and stared at him, waiting for his answer.

"I—I suppose, if I wanted to—"

"Then want to. If you'll spend from December the nineteenth to midnight, December the twenty-fifth, with me, doing whatever I ask of you, and you still want the divorce, I'll give it to you, uncontested."

"Like—do what?"

"Like I said—whatever I ask. That should be simple enough, and remember, your children will be with you some of that time. If you go ahead with the divorce proceedings now, you know they won't have a thing at all to do with you over the holidays. This way, you'll be able to have a lovely Christmas with them, then file for divorce after Christmas is over." *That also means you won't be able to see your little cutie during that time, but I'm not going to mention that now and start another argument. I want you home for Christmas.*

"The children still don't know?"

She shook her head. "Only Buck. He came back about an hour after you left me on Thanksgiving Day. He'd left his wallet in the bathroom. I'm afraid I was in pretty bad shape. I had to tell him, but I made him promise not to say anything to anyone other than Shonna. I'm sure he's kept that promise. He's not happy about this, Randy, but for DeeDee and Aaron's sake, I'm sure he'll treat you civilly. At least until December the twenty-sixth."

"You're making this really tough, Syl." Randy leaned back in his chair, locking his hands behind his head and closing his eyes.

She knew her offer had come as a shock. "I don't plan to

place all the blame on you when the kids are told. I'm sure I had a part in the failure of our marriage, too. I—I may not have been the wife you wanted me to be, but I did try."

"This is the craziest idea I've ever heard! I will *not* move back home, even for a single night!"

She worked hard at maintaining her cool. He had to say yes. She was counting on it. *Don't blow it now!* "It'd be a way to avoid a knockdown, drag-out in court."

"If you kept your end of the bargain."

"I guess you'll have to trust me," she answered, willing her voice to remain calm, at least on the surface. "Randy? What do you say? If you want this divorce, you'd better make up your mind real fast. Once I walk out that door, you can consider this offer withdrawn, and our lawyers can handle everything. Take it or leave it."

He inhaled a couple of quick breaths.

"Make up your mind, Randy. Think how nice it'd be to have at least one more peaceful Christmas with the kids."

"But what good would spending another week under the same roof accomplish?"

She glanced at her watch. "Time's a wasting."

Looking pressured, he leaned forward and folded his hands on the desktop. "You know this is only going to prolong things."

"Perhaps."

"And I'm supposed to move back into the house during that time?"

"Yes. I want your undivided attention every minute of those seven days. It's a small sacrifice if you want to avoid a nasty divorce court battle."

"You're leaving me no choice, you know."

"That was my intent."

Agitated, he rose and began to pace about the room, frantically running his fingers through his hair. Finally coming to a stop in front of her, he leaned toward her, his voice shaking with emotion. "Look, Sylvia, we've been living separate lives for years. The only thing we haven't done is the paperwork making it official. This whole thing seems a bit silly to me."

She wanted to shout at him, but she held her peace, pulling out the one last card left in her deck. Moving to the other side of the desk, she gave him a smile as she shrugged, slung the strap of her purse over her shoulder, and headed for the door. "Okay. If you'd rather do things your way, I'll see you in court."

She had only taken a few steps when Randy grabbed her arm and spun her around.

"All right, you win. I'll do it, but I'm not happy about it."

She pulled her arm from his grasp. "Sorry, that's one of the conditions of the deal. You at least have to act as if you're happy about it. I won't have you sulking around our house like a spoiled child who didn't get his way. Christmas is a happy time, Randy. The celebration of the birth of our Savior, Jesus Christ. I won't have you ruining it with a downtrodden face and a smart mouth."

He lifted both palms with a look of defeat. "Okay, okay. We'll do it your way."

Her heart did a flip-flop. Randy was going to agree! "You'll at least act like you're enjoying being home for Christmas?"

"Yeah, if you're a good sport about this, I guess I need to be one, too."

She had to get out of there before she shouted *Hallelujah!* "Good, I'll expect you in time for supper on December the nineteenth, and don't be late. No excuses, Randy, or the deal's off. Have everything taken care of at the office by the nineteenth. No running to the paper. No meeting with clients. None of that. Because if that happens, like I said, I'll see you in court, and I can assure you it won't be a pretty sight. I'll take you for everything I can get!"

He gave her a guarded smile. "You drive a hard bargain. I didn't know you had it in you."

She grabbed hold of the doorknob and smiled over her shoulder. "Only when my marriage is at stake, then I can be a wildcat!" She did an exaggerated Meee—ooow, showed her claws, then moved out and closed the door behind her.

"I'm so glad you came, Mrs. Benson," Carol told her from her place at her desk. "Mr. Benson has seemed a little down the past few days. I'm sure your surprise visit cheered him up."

"I—I hope so." Sylvia had to smile. *If you only knew, Carol.*

ભ

For the next couple of weeks, Sylvia rushed about like a mad woman on a mission, cleaning the house until it sparkled, readying their bedroom for Randy's return, shopping for Christmas presents, and a to-do list full of other things. She was busy from early morning until late at night, and for the first time in days—happy. She'd even printed out a small banner on her computer's printer saying, "Give her of the fruit of her hands; and let her own works praise her in the gates," and taped it on the mirror in her bathroom as a reminder, claiming that verse as her own, confident God had given it to her. She made out a carefully choreographed schedule for each day Randy would be with her and planned the important activities they would do together. Just knowing Randy was going to be back home with her, even for a few days, made her feel giddy and young again. How long had it been since she had planned something special for just the two of them? Too long!

Each night as she knelt beside her bed and prayed in Jesus' name, she asked God to give her wisdom and guidance and for the strength to keep her mouth shut when the need arose. It would be so easy to tear into her husband about Chatalaine, but now that she was convinced that her own negligence and not just Chatalaine's youth and good looks threatened to end her marriage, she found it easier to put the woman out of her mind. She needed to concentrate on herself and the devotion and dedication she had pledged to Randy on their wedding day.

Other than talking to Jen and Buck, she kept things to herself. At first, Buck was skeptical of her plan. He felt she was getting her hopes up and did not want to see her hurt anymore than she'd already been hurt. But at her request, he and Shonna agreed to go along with her plan and to treat his father as if nothing had happened.

Finally, December the nineteenth arrived. Sylvia spent part of the morning at the beauty shop having her long hair cut into a pixie style with wisps of hair feathering her face. "You look years younger," the beauty operator had told her as she gave her the hand mirror and swung her chair around. "I left a few wisps along your neckline, too. I think you'll like it that way."

Sylvia had gazed into the mirror and had to agree. The style did make her look several years younger. She was sure Randy would like it.

She was too excited to eat lunch and opted for a banana and a glass of cranberry juice. By two o'clock, she had baked a lemon meringue pie, piling the heavily beaten egg whites high and creating curly mounds just like Randy liked them. She hadn't baked a lemon meringue pie since she'd made one for the Fourth of July picnic at the church, although Randy had always claimed it was his favorite dessert. When she pulled the pie from the oven and placed it on the counter to cool, she looked at the deliciously browned meringue and experienced terrible pangs of guilt. Why hadn't she baked more of those pies for Randy? The children loved them, too. They took no time at all. She had baked several of them to take to the church bake sales, but had not made a single one for him in years.

By four, the table was set with the stoneware she usually reserved for company. The few freshly cut flowers she'd purchased at the market had been arranged in a colorful vase as a centerpiece, the crab casserole he liked was in the oven baking, and everything was in readiness. All she had to do was take her shower and get dressed.

When the phone rang a few minutes later, she cringed. *Randy, if that's you calling to say you're going to be late or that you can't make it, I'm going to be furious.*

"Hello."

"Hi," Jen said on the other end. "I just want you to know I've been praying for you all day, and I'm going to keep praying right on through Christmas Day."

Sylvia's heart soared. With a praying friend like Jen, how could things not go right? "Thanks, Jen. You don't know how much that means to me. I'm as nervous as I was on our first date."

"You'll do fine, honey. Just be your natural sweet self."

Sylvia huffed. "You wouldn't have thought I was sweet if you'd heard me threatening Randy in his office that day. I wasn't about to take no for an answer. Jen, I know God gave me that verse."

"I know it, too, and I think your plan is marvelous. If Randy doesn't see what he's giving up by the time Christmas Day arrives, I'll be mighty surprised."

"I'm counting on that. I don't even want to think about failing."

"You won't fail. Not with both of us praying about it. God knows your heart, Sylvia, and He knows the two of you belong together."

Sylvia thanked her for praying, said good-bye, and rushed up the stairs to take her shower.

❧

Randy stared into the mirror at the stubble on his cheeks and chin. Like his father, he had been blessed with a head of thick hair, but with it came the proverbial five o'clock shadow.

What a week he'd had. It seemed everything that could go wrong—did. Two of his key employees quit to go to work for the state government, where they would get better benefits. One of the main presses broke down as they were running the "Dallas Life" section for the Sunday paper, and Carol had tripped on the stairs and broken her arm. To top it all off, his rechargeable razor had quit on him when he had started to shave, and now he was going to have to use the emergency disposable razor he kept in his shaving kit. The way things were going, he would probably cut himself.

Well, trouble or not, he had taken off a bit early to get ready to move back into the house for the next week, and he was committed to going through with it. The paper would have to get along without him for a while. The only good thing going for him was his assistant manager, a young man who showed great promise. Randy had spent most of the day going over last-minute details with him, and, hopefully, the guy would be able to handle any crisis that might develop in his absence. Sylvia had made it perfectly clear she wasn't about to accept any excuses that would take him away from her for the next week, and he certainly did not want to end up in an expensive court battle if he could avoid it.

It was hard to believe she hadn't made any attempt to contact him since that day she'd appeared in his office, other than to send him a short handwritten note reminding him she'd be looking for him at six that evening. He had expected her to call him at the office continually, bemoaning the fact that he had asked for the divorce, but she had not, and he appreciated it. Maybe they *could* get through this divorce without all the hullabaloo he had expected, after all. He should be so lucky.

He jumped when his cell phone rang, almost afraid to answer it for fear there had been another fiasco at the newspaper.

"Hi, Randy," a male voice on the other end said pleasantly. "I have a favor to ask."

Randy recognized the man's voice immediately. It was Bill Regier, a fellow deacon.

"I know you've been so busy at the newspaper you haven't been able to attend church the past few Sundays, but my wife is insisting we go visit her folks over New Year's, and I wondered if I could talk you into teaching my junior high Sunday school class? They're a great bunch of kids, and I know they'll like you."

Teach Sunday school? Me? When I've just asked my wife for a divorce? Randy rubbed his free hand up the stubble on his jaw. "I—I don't think so, Bill. I've been kinda out of the loop lately—you know—with too many things going on in my life. It's a busy time of year, and—"

"Hey, this isn't rocket science. It won't take that much preparation. You can just tell the kids how you came to Christ. You know, when you accepted Jesus and what's happened in your life since. It'll be an inspiration for them. These kids need role models in their lives. Some of them are from the bus ministry and come from broken homes. They need to see what a real man is like. A man like you—with values and principles."

Randy was glad their conversation was on the phone so the man couldn't see his face—a face he was sure betrayed his guilt. "I—I'd like to help you out, Bill, but—but I'm afraid I can't do it this time. Year-end stuff, you know?"

There was a pause on the other end, then, "Well, okay, but it's these kids' loss. Maybe another time, when you're not so busy, huh?"

"Yeah—maybe another time." Randy tapped the OFF button, but continued to stare at the receiver. *Role model, Bill? You won't think so when you hear about the divorce.*

❧

Sylvia opened the Dillard's shopping bag and dumped the assortment of new cosmetics she had purchased several days ago onto the dresser. She'd never worn much makeup, never thought she'd need to, but after seeing the beautiful Chatalaine in the restaurant that day, she'd felt dowdy and washed out. Colorless. The woman at the department store's makeup counter had been extremely helpful and had given her all kinds of tips on applying moisturizer, foundation, blusher, eyeliner, mascara, and even lip-liner. Now, if she could just remember all she had learned. *Beauty is only skin-deep,* the old saying her mother used to quote, popped into her mind as she gazed at herself in the mirror. She let out an audible giggle as a second quote came to mind. This one she had heard while playing one of Billy Graham's videotapes. *Every old barn can use a little paint now and then!*

"Well, this old barn certainly can!" she chided as she picked up the bottle of moisturizer. She began to apply it freely to her scrubbed-clean skin. After smoothing on the foundation and blusher, she picked up the eyeliner pencil and, using a finger to pull each eyelid tautly to one side, she carefully made a narrow line, one above and one below her lashes on each eye. *Umm, not bad for a beginner!* Next came the mascara, something she rarely used. "One light coat, let it dry a few seconds, then apply a second coat more freely," the woman had said. Once that was done, she reached for one of the new lip-liner pencils she'd purchased and chose one in a deep mauve shade. "Frame your mouth, staying right on the very edge of the lip line," she could almost hear the beauty consultant say as she applied it. She had never used lip liner before, but she had to admit, it did define her lips. Next, she reached for the mauve lipstick, in a shade a bit lighter than the liner. Sylvia applied it generously, then blotted it carefully on a tissue before looking back into the mirror. The woman who smiled back at her looked nothing like the woman who'd faced her in that same mirror the day before. What an improvement!

"Man looketh on the outward appearance, but the Lord looketh on the heart!" The words she had committed to memory so many years ago echoed in her heart. *I haven't forgotten that, God, but I want to look my very best for Randy. I want to knock his socks off!*

She spritzed her hair with the setting mist and used her fingers to lift and separate the wisps, pulling a few of them toward her face, just like the beautician had shown her when she'd cut her hair. A few puffs of hair spray, the addition of her new gold hoop earrings and a fine gold chain about her neck, and she was ready to slip into the gorgeous, rose-printed silk caftan she'd bought for their first evening together. She had already done her fingernails and toenails in the same rosy-mauve color. She gave herself a quick spray of the perfume Randy had given her for Christmas two years ago—the one she'd never even bothered to open. Then she slipped into her gold, heelless sandals, took one last glimpse at the mirror, and headed downstairs. She felt giddy, almost like a fairy princess on her way to the ball. Now if only Randy would behave as she imagined Prince Charming would behave. She laughed aloud as she whirled her way into the kitchen for a few last-minute preparations, visualizing Randy appearing at her door dressed in all white with gold braid at his shoulders and astride a fine white horse.

She turned on the coffeepot, checked the oven, gave the salad another toss, shifted the fresh flower vase a half inch to make sure it was centered just right, then moved into the living room to await his arrival.

At exactly six, the doorbell rang. She straightened, her heart pounding. If it was Randy, why didn't he simply use his key? After all, this *was* his home.

seven

Randy stared at the door, suitcase and garment bag in hand. Maybe he should have just used his key and gone in rather than ringing the doorbell like a visitor. But he *was* a visitor! He had moved out of this home he had known and loved. He glanced toward the west, to the three-bedroom addition they had added nearly twenty years ago, after DeeDee and Aaron became toddlers. He looked to the east at the big bay windows of the family room where the garage used to be. How they had needed that extra space when the kids started school and began bringing their friends over. Fortunately, their house had been on a corner lot, making it possible for them to expand the kitchen and build a nice attached three-car garage onto the backside of the house.

He remembered when they had nearly sold this home and simply bought a larger one in another neighborhood, but both Sylvia and the kids had wanted to stay where they were, near all the friends they had made and their church. As the managing editor of the newspaper, he could well afford to buy a bigger house now, but this home had always filled their needs. It was warm and comfortable, thanks to Sylvia and her decorating talents.

Realization smacked him between the eyes as the door opened and Sylvia appeared. He no longer lived here. He *was* a visitor!

&

"Hi," Sylvia said, her voice cracking slightly with pent-up emotion. "Come on in." She watched Randy move through the door and place his things in the hall. It was obvious he was feeling every bit as awkward as she was.

He gazed at her, looking first at her hair, then her face, then the new caftan she was wearing. She liked the look she saw in his eyes. Though she felt herself trembling, she willed her voice to remain pleasant and calm. "Supper is nearly ready. Would you like a glass of iced tea or maybe a cup of coffee?"

"Ah—no. Nothing, thanks."

She laughed within herself as she gave him a purposely demure smile. He was wearing a burgundy knit polo shirt that nearly matched the dark burgundy lines surrounding the huge mauve roses in the print of her caftan.

"You've cut your hair," he said, his eyes still focused on her. "I like it."

A flash of warmth rushed to her cheeks at his compliment. "Thank you. I like it, too. The hairdresser said it made me look years younger." *That was a stupid thing to say!*

"It does."

But not as young as your precious Chatalaine?

She gestured toward the living room and his recliner. "Would you like to sit down? I put a couple of your favorite CDs on to play." *Christian CDs. Or don't you like that kind anymore?*

"Sure. I guess."

He followed her into the living room and sat down in what used to be his chair. "Pretty dress. I guess you'd call it a dress. Looks good on you."

She lowered herself gracefully onto the chintz sofa and smoothed at the long caftan. "Thank you."

"It's new? I've never seen it before."

"Yes, new." *I bought it to impress you, hoping you'd like it.*

"How are the kids? I haven't heard from any of them."

"They're fine. DeeDee and Aaron are working hard on

finals. Buck and Shonna are busy getting ready for Christmas. He's working lots of overtime." *Buck is furious with you! And DeeDee and Aaron will be, too, when they hear you're deserting your family for that woman!*

"I guess—you're doing okay. You look wonderful."

Doing okay? No, I'm not doing okay! I'm awful! I can't sleep, can't eat, cry all day and all night. I'm miserable without you! "I'm—managing. Thank you for the compliment. How are you doing?"

"Okay. Busy. At the office, you know. Busy time of the year."

"Yes, I remember," she said, fully aware of his rigid position. *He must be feeling as awkward in my presence as I feel in his. Two strangers, instead of a man and woman who've been married for twenty-five years and have three grown children.* "How is your apartment working out?"

"Other than hearing the elevator go up and down all night, it's working out fine. I need to get some furniture. The place is still pretty empty."

"Is it near your office?" She had wondered where he had moved, but he had never even given her a hint, let alone the address.

"About a mile. I could walk it, I guess. On nice days."

They sat in silence, listening to a gospel medley about God's love, each avoiding the other's eyes.

"I—I think the casserole should be done by now," Sylvia said, rising. "It's your favorite."

"Not the crab casserole you used to bake for me?"

The enthusiasm on his face made her smile. "Yes. The crab casserole."

He rose and rubbed his hands together briskly. "Sounds like I'm in for a treat!"

She crooked a finger at him, adding the demure smile once

again, and headed for the kitchen, knowing he was following at her heels.

"Umm, does that smell good." He made an exaggerated sniff at the air. "I can't remember the last time you made that casserole."

"Far too long ago." *I'm ashamed to admit.*

He moved into his usual chair as she pulled the casserole from the oven and placed it on the iron trivet on the table. "Need any help?"

She shook her head. "No, I just need to get our salad bowls from the refrigerator, and we'll be ready to eat." Once the salad bowls were set in place, she lowered herself into her chair and bowed her head. Normally, Randy prayed at suppertime, but after a few moments of silence, she prayed aloud, a simple prayer thanking God for their food and asking Him to be with their family. She wanted to thank God audibly for bringing Randy back home, but felt it better left unsaid. At least aloud. The last thing she wanted to do was make him feel uncomfortable. She wanted to "let her works praise her in the gates"—her own home.

When she lifted her eyes, she found Randy staring at her. Was it a look of admiration, or resentment, or even tolerance? She couldn't tell. All she could do was her very best to make him see what he was giving up by moving out. One last look at the life they had shared. *Oh, God, make him want to come home for good! Please make him want to come home.*

She offered him the serving spoon. "Go ahead and help yourself while I get the rolls from the oven."

"This looks wonderful," he told her, scooping a huge serving from the casserole dish. "I wasn't sure you even remembered it was my favorite."

I remembered, Randy, I just didn't care, I guess. I always fixed the things the kids liked, putting your wants and needs aside. You never complained. I just figured it wasn't important. "I remembered."

He took the first bite and chewed it slowly, appearing to savor it by the looks of his contented smile. "I know the kids never liked crab. I sure couldn't have expected you to go to all the trouble to fix the crab casserole for me. You had enough to do."

"I like it, too. I wish now I *had* fixed it for you."

He looked up, his dark eyes fixed on her. "I do, too, Sylvia."

"Have a roll. They're nice and hot," she said quickly, needing to change the subject.

"Thanks."

"Are you ready for coffee?"

He sent a gentle smile her way and pointed to her still empty plate. "Eat, Sylvia, while everything is hot. I can wait on the coffee. The water is fine."

They finished their supper in near silence, their only conversation forced. Sylvia tried to relax, but it was hard. She wanted to throw herself into Randy's arms and beg him to come back to her.

When they had finished and nearly all the casserole was gone, Randy leaned back in the chair with a satisfied sigh, linking his fingers across his chest. "That's the best meal I've had in a long time. Thanks, Sylvia."

"You're welcome." She gave him an impish grin. "If you had your choice of desserts, what would it be?"

"Lemon meringue pie, of course," he answered without hesitation. "Don't tell me—"

"Yes," she said smiling with pride as she rose and pulled her beautiful pie from the cabinet. "Lemon meringue pie." For a moment, she thought Randy was going to cry. The look he gave her was one she had not seen in a long time, and it tugged at her heartstrings.

"I know you're doing all these nice things in hope I'll change my mind—about the divorce—but, Sylvia, I am going to go through with it. I don't want you to get the idea that things are going to change just because you've fixed my favorite foods."

Now *she* wanted to cry, but instead, she pasted on a smile. "Let's not discuss the divorce. For this week, that word is off-limits. We made a deal, remember? And I plan to honor my end of the bargain. Give me this one week, Randy, as you've promised. This one last Christmas together, okay?"

He nodded, and she could tell his smile was as false as hers.

"Good, let's enjoy our pie." She cut generous wedges for each of them, then filled their coffee cups.

"Oh, babe, that's good," Randy said, taking his first bite. Then he seemed embarrassed that he had called her *babe*, the pet name he had used the first few years of their marriage.

She ignored his embarrassment as she forked up her own bite of the delicious pie. She had to admit it was one of the best lemon meringue pies she had ever baked. She hadn't lost her touch. "I'm glad you're enjoying it, Randy. I'd hoped you would."

"I guess I should offer to help load the dishwasher," he said, placing his fork on his plate and folding up his napkin.

"I'd like that." Normally, before she had gone off to college, DeeDee helped her mother with the clearing of the table and the dishwasher loading. To her recollection, Randy had never helped with the dishes. He had been too busy with his studies the first four years of their marriage. After he graduated, he had worked at two jobs to make ends meet so she could quit work and stay home to raise their family. Since that time, she had always been a stay-at-home mom, and he had never needed to take part in household chores.

Maybe he should have! Then he'd have a better idea of what I've been doing for this family all these years. Things, apparently, he's taken for granted.

He gave her an I-really-didn't-mean-it smile, stood, and began stacking up their plates and silverware. "You'll have to show me how to do it."

"It's quite simple." She took the plates and silverware from him and rinsed them off under the faucet before handing them back to him. "Plates stand on end in those little slots on the bottom shelf. Silverware goes in the basket. Glasses and cups upside-down on the top shelf, saucers same place as the plates."

She watched him awkwardly place the dishes where she had told him. "One capful of dish soap goes in the dispenser, then swing the lid closed, shut the door, and latch it."

Once the dishwasher was in operation and the rest of the table cleared, with things put where they belonged in the cabinets and refrigerator, she shook the tablecloth, stuffed it into the laundry basket in the utility room, and placed the colorful basket of silk flowers back on the table. "That's that! Let's go into the family room. A letter came in today's mail from DeeDee addressed to both of us. I haven't opened it yet."

He followed her, heading for the cushy green leather recliner—his recliner. But he stopped midroom as if remembering the last time he had tried to sit in that chair and she had chastised him, saying he no longer belonged in it.

"Go ahead," she said, trying to sound unconcerned, but remembering that same incident as vividly as if it had happened that very evening. "We bought it especially for you. Remember?"

He moved into the chair cautiously, settling himself down and propping up the footrest.

Sylvia watched with great interest, wishing she had a camera to capture his picture. He belonged in that chair, in this house, not in some high-rise apartment. She pulled a footstool up close to his chair and opened the note from their daughter, reading it aloud.

Dear Mom and Dad,

I was sitting here in my room, listening to my roommate complain about her parents, and I suddenly realized how lucky I am to have been born to the two of you. Mom, you're the greatest. You always put your kids' needs ahead of your own and were always there for us, doing the little things that made our childhood so happy and carefree.

Sylvia's heart swelled with happiness at her daughter's words. She went on without so much as a sideways glance at Randy. She knew one look in his direction and she'd lose it.

Dad, you work too hard. I wish you hadn't had to spend so much time at the newspaper, and I know I used to gripe about it all the time, especially when you had to miss my volleyball and basketball games. But now that I am older, I realize you did it because you loved me, and you wanted to provide all the things for us kids that you never had and to be able to send Buck and Aaron and me to college.

Sylvia was sure she heard a distinct sigh coming from the cushy green leather chair, but she read on, sure their daughter's words were affecting him as much as they were her.

I've never thanked you two properly, but I want you to know I love you both and appreciate you and everything you've done for me. If my life ever amounts to anything, it'll be because of the two of you and the way you love the Lord and the witness you have been to me. Maybe now that Aaron and I are gone, you two can do some of the things you've put on hold while we were growing up. I pray for you every day, asking God to protect you and keep you both well. I'll see you December twenty-fourth. With love, your daughter, DeeDee.

When she finished, she folded the note and slipped it back into its envelope, not sure what to say or if she should just remain quiet. When Randy didn't speak, she rose, crossed the room, and placed the envelope on the coffee table.

"She's—she's a great kid, isn't she?" he finally asked, after clearing his throat.

"Yes, she is. All three of our kids are great kids."

"You've done a good job with them. I'm—I'm afraid I can't take much of the credit."

She moved back to the footstool and seated herself, smiling up at him, ignoring the ache in her heart. "I wouldn't have been able to be a stay-at-home mom if you hadn't worked so hard to provide for us."

"But it took me away from home. I missed the kids' games, their school activities, so many things."

She gave his arm a tender pat. "But you were at church with us most Sundays, and you've served faithfully on the church board all these years.

"You—you still haven't told them—about—"

"No, I haven't, and I'm sure Buck hasn't either, and I don't intend to, Randy. When and if the time comes, you'll have to be the one to do it."

He leaned his head against the headrest and stared off in space. "It is going to happen, Sylvia. I've been thinking about this for a long time. I nearly asked you for a divorce last summer, before you and the kids went to Colorado to attend that Christian camp, but I thought it might be easier on everyone if I waited until DeeDee and Aaron went off to college."

"Easier on them? Or easier on you?" she prodded gently, wishing right away she had kept her question to herself. "Don't answer that," she added quickly. "We're putting all that behind us now. I had no business even asking."

He gave her a faint smile, then closed his eyes. "This chair is comfortable. Feels like it was made for me."

She reached out and pulled his shoe off, and when he didn't protest, she pulled the other one off and placed them on the floor beside the chair. "I know."

"The music's nice."

"I thought you'd like it."

For the next few hours, they sat listening to the stack of CDs she had put on the player. Randy in his recliner, Sylvia stretched out on the chintz sofa. As the last song played and the room became silent, Sylvia heard a faint snore coming from the recliner. Randy was fast asleep.

She tiptoed into the hall, quietly picked up his suitcase and garment bag, and carried them up the stairs and into their room. She hung his garments in his nearly empty closet, then placed his suitcase on the bench at the end of the bed. She nearly unpacked it for him—and would have before their separation. But now it seemed like an invasion of his privacy, and she did not want to upset him by doing something that might offend him.

After washing her face and reapplying a faint trace of the rose-colored lipstick, she rubbed a sweet-smelling body lotion on her face and arms and slipped into the pink, lacy gown she had bought when she had been shopping for the other items she planned to wear during their week together. Before she left the room, she fell to her knees by the bed and asked God to be with the two of them and to give her the grace to be patient, loving, and kind. Lastly, she asked Him to keep her from saying things she shouldn't and to bring Randy back home for good—home where he belonged.

He was still sleeping in the chair when she came back into the family room, his head twisted to one side, his arms resting on the armrests. He looked like a little boy, and she wanted to kiss his sweet face. She could not remember the last time he had fallen asleep in that chair.

"Randy," she said softly, giving his shoulder an easy shake. "It's nearly eleven. Time to go to bed."

He sat up with a start, blinking as if he had to get his bearings. "How—how long have I been asleep?"

She reached out and gave his hand a tug. "Probably an hour."

He lowered the footrest and allowed her to pull him to his feet. "I—I'll get my things," he said, heading toward the front hall.

"They're already in our room."

He gave her a wild stare. "I—I was planning on sleeping in the guest room."

"This is still your home, Randy, at least until midnight Christmas Day. You'll be sleeping in our bed tonight, where you belong."

eight

He backed away from her, holding his palms up between them. "I—I don't think so."

She stepped toward him, determined to make her plans work out as she had envisioned them. "We *do* have a king-sized bed. There's plenty of room for both of us. I'll sleep on my side. You sleep on yours."

When he did not respond with more than a doubtful grunt, she added, trying to keep her voice sweet and on an even keel, "You do plan to keep your part of the bargain, don't you?"

He gave a defeated shrug and headed for the stairs without answering. As soon as he reached their room, he unzipped his suitcase and pulled out what looked to be a brand new pair of pajamas, still bearing the creases from their packaging. Sylvia muffled a laugh. Although she'd bought him a number of pairs of nice men's pajamas during the years they'd been married, he'd always refused to wear them, opting for a T-shirt and boxers, saying only old men in hospitals or care homes wore pajamas.

She waited patiently, sitting on her side of the bed while he showered, using the time to read her Bible. Minutes later he emerged, his curly hair damp, and wearing the new pajamas. "Shower feel good?"

He nodded. "Yeah, I've always loved that big showerhead. Makes a guy feel really clean."

Is that a faint tinge of aftershave I smell? Did he put that on just for me? "I like that showerhead, too, especially when I rinse my hair," she added, closing her Bible. "I put a glass of water on your nightstand."

He glanced toward the glass. "Thanks."

"I'm not going to bite, Randy," she told him, giving him a raise of her brow.

"I—I know, I just feel—awkward, that's all, now that things are—different—between us."

"I still love you," she reminded him gently, not wanting to add to his discomfort.

He took a swig of the water, set the glass back in the coaster, and lowered himself onto his side of the bed, keeping his back toward her.

Sylvia quickly scooted across the bed on her knees and cupped her hands on his shoulders. Although he flinched and gave her a what-are-you-doing look, he did not move away. "You've been working too hard. Let me rub your shoulders."

"You don't have—"

"I know I don't have to—I want to. Now sit still." She began gently kneading his deltoid muscles, letting her fingers perform their magic.

"Umm, that feels so good."

"You're way too tense, Randy. Come on, relax."

"I don't want you to tire yourself."

"I'll quit when I get tired. Now let me work those neck muscles."

He bowed his head low and, oohing and aahing with each stroke, he let her fingertips press into his strong neck.

"I used to do this when we were first married, when you came home from your classes, remember?" she asked, leaning against him.

He nodded. "Yeah, I remember. Knowing you'd be waiting for me at the end of a hard day at college, ready to massage my weariness away, was what kept me going those last few hours."

Finally, he reached up and took hold of her hand. "Stop.

That's enough. As much as I'm enjoying it, I don't want you to get hand cramps."

She leaned over his back and planted a kiss on his cheek before scooting back over onto her side of the bed and slipping under the quilt. As he turned to look at her, she flipped back his side of the covers, then turned her back to him. "Good night, Randy."

She felt the bed move slightly as he crawled in, pulled up the covers, and turned out the light on his nightstand. "Good night, Syl."

Sylvia arose early the next morning and carefully slipped out from under the covers, leaving Randy sprawled on his side of the bed, tangled up in the sheet and quilt. She had to smile. Parts of his thick hair stood in mounds where he had gone to sleep with it wet from his shower.

She wiggled into the new pair of jeans she had bought and topped them with a bright fuchsia T-shirt, a color she never wore. Most of her life, she had opted for beige, white, or soft pastel colors, never gaudy ones. But this week called for extreme measures, so many of the new things she'd bought were way out of her usual color realm, colors more like what she thought Chatalaine would wear.

Chatalaine.

She was glad Randy had not mentioned that woman's name. She did not plan to, either. The less he thought about Chatalaine, the better, as far as she was concerned. She had him on her turf now, and she planned to keep him there all week.

After spritzing her newly cut hair and finger combing it as the beautician had shown her, she painstakingly applied her new makeup and added another dash of Randy's perfume. By the time he arrived in the kitchen, also dressed in jeans and a T-shirt, the table had been set and she had breakfast well underway. "Good morning," she called out cheerily. "I hope you slept well."

He ran his fingers through the hair at his temples. "Extremely well. I like that mattress. The one I have at the—"

She put a finger to his lips on her way to the refrigerator, silencing him. "We're not going to talk about your apartment this week," she said as she pulled the bottle of cranberry juice from the fridge and filled their glasses. "The bacon is ready, and I'll put the eggs-in-a-basket on a platter as soon as we've prayed, so they'll be good and hot. Would you pour the coffee?"

He moved to the coffeemaker, lifted the pot, and filled their cups. "Umm, that smells good. New jeans?"

She froze. She had bought the faded ones purposely so he would not think they were brand new. "I haven't had them very long."

"Nice T-shirt."

"I've decided I like bright colors."

"Looks good on you."

Sylvia smiled, then bowed her head and prayed. Though he usually prayed at breakfast, she knew he must feel awkward doing it under the circumstances, and she wanted him to be at ease.

"I thought we'd take a walk after breakfast," she said lightly as she placed her napkin in her lap.

He picked up his fork with a quizzical look. "Oh? Where to?"

She grinned. "You'll see."

"Ah, Syl?"

"Yes?"

"Could—could I have a piece of that pie for breakfast before we leave?"

They finished their breakfast, pulled on their jackets, and headed out the kitchen door and through the garage. Randy seemed surprised when Sylvia stopped and opened her car door.

"I thought you said we were going for a walk."

She motioned him inside, crawled in herself, and hit the button on the garage door opener. "Too boring to walk around here. I thought we'd walk around the Lakeside Park area. It's pretty over there."

He closed the door and buckled his seatbelt. "I haven't been to that area in years."

"I know."

It was a beautiful day. The sun was shining, and there were just enough breezes to make the leaves on the trees sway gently. Sylvia parked the car along the curb, and they set out walking.

"You don't have your cell phone on your belt," she said almost jubilantly.

"I didn't think you wanted me getting any calls."

She grinned. "I don't, but I don't want you to cut yourself off totally, in case there is an emergency at the newspaper."

"I think things will be all right. That young man I told you about should be able to—"

"You never told me about any young man."

His pace slowed and his brows rose. "I didn't?"

"No, you didn't, but I'm glad you have someone to help you at the paper. You've needed a dependable assistant for a long time."

"I hate turning things over to someone else."

"I know."

"Did I tell you Carol broke her arm?"

She stopped walking as her jaw dropped. "No! When did that happen?"

"Yesterday. About noon. I had to take her to the hospital. It happened right after they called and told me one of our big presses went down."

Guilt hit her like a Mack truck. "Oh, Randy, I'm so sorry to hear that. What a day you must've had. Is she okay? Did you get the presses rolling?"

"I guess she'll be all right when the swelling goes down. She'll be off at least until after New Year's, but she still won't be able to type when she comes back. I'll have to hire a temp to help her. And no, the presses were still down when I left the office, but two guys from the company that sold it to us are flying down from Cincinnati to help get it back in operation." He took a few more steps, then turned to her again. "I guess I didn't tell you two of my key men in the newsroom quit this week. They got jobs with the State Department. They gave them much better benefits than I could offer. I don't blame them, but it sure left me high and dry. They were good men."

Her eyes widened. "No, you didn't tell me about them. Oh, Randy, I had no idea how hard it was for you to take this entire week off. If you need to call the office——"

He placed his hand on her arm. "No, they aren't expecting a call from me. I've told everyone *not* to call me, short of a real emergency. I've put the newspaper first in my life for way too long. From now on, I'm looking out for Number One. Me. I'm going to do the things I've always wanted to and never had the time or the money."

Like buy a motorcycle and wear gold chains around your neck?

"I may even take up golf, or fishing, maybe even hunting. I haven't decided yet. I might even do some traveling."

Alone? Please don't tell me you plan to take Chatalaine with you!

"I've even considering taking flying lessons; maybe buy myself a small plane."

"My, you do have plans. I hadn't realized you were interested in any of those things."

"Most of them were only pipe dreams—things I wanted to do when I retired, but too many men I know—guys my age—

have been dropping like flies. Never even making it into their sixties. I don't want to be one of them."

Is that what this is all about? Your mortality?

"My dad died just a few months before his sixtieth birthday, his dad in his late fifties. I want to do things while I'm in good enough health to enjoy them, and I figure now's as good a time as any. From what my older acquaintances tell me, it ain't gonna get any better."

You are in a midlife crisis! "But your grandfather on your mother's side is still alive, and he's in his eighties!" she countered. "That's in your favor."

"But my body is much more like my father's side of the family."

Sylvia grabbed his hand and tugged him toward a nearby park bench. She sat and pulled him down beside her. "No one is invincible, Randy. Only God knows when He's going to call us home."

Randy ignored her comment as he looked around, taking in the park, the chip-lined walking path, and the park bench itself. "Hey, this is all beginning to look very familiar," he said, eyeing her with a laugh. "We didn't just happen to stumble onto this particular bench, did we?"

Her heart rose like a kite caught in an updraft. "You remembered!"

"I proposed to you in this very spot nearly twenty-six years ago."

"Yes, you did. And I gladly accepted your proposal, Randy. You're the only man I've ever loved. That little diamond you placed on my finger that day was the most beautiful ring I had ever seen. I'll never forget how excited I was. I was going to be Mrs. Randy Benson!"

"Boy, were we naive. A couple of kids who had no idea what we were doing or what the future held for us."

She cupped her hand on his shoulder and smiled into his deep blue eyes. "A couple of kids in love who were willing to face anything to be together."

"Your parents weren't too happy when they saw that ring on your finger as I recall."

"No, they much preferred that I attend college and get a degree in nursing, but marrying you was all I wanted out of life. Once they realized that, they accepted it." She scooted a tad closer to him. "Our life and our marriage may not have been perfect, but I never wanted it to end."

He stood quickly and glanced at his watch. "Hey, it's nearly noon. I'm hungry; how about you?"

"Sounds good to me, and I know just the place to have lunch."

She took his hand and led him across the street and down two blocks, to the little all-night diner where they used to eat hotdogs when they could afford to splurge and eat out.

Randy opened the door and stood back to allow her entrance. "Boy, I didn't even know this place was still in business."

"Then you do remember coming here?"

He nodded, stepping inside. "Yeah, I remember. You were pregnant with Buck, and you continually seemed to have a craving for foot-long hotdogs with pickle relish and loads of mustard. I wonder if they still have them on their menu."

They crowded into the only booth that was available, a small single-sided bench in the far corner.

"Yep, they're still on the menu! You up to it?" Randy asked when the waitress brought their water glasses.

Sylvia smiled back at him. "You bet!"

They giggled through lunch like two junior high kids, consuming their hotdogs and even ordering chocolate shakes to go with them.

"I'm stuffed," Randy said on their way back to where they

had parked the car. "Why didn't you tell me to stop when I ordered that second hotdog?"

"Would you have listened?" she answered, slipping her hand into his as they walked along.

He gave it a slight squeeze, but did not pull away. "Probably not!"

When they reached the car, Sylvia handed Randy her keys. "You drive."

He opened her door and waited until she was safely inside before jogging around to the driver's side. "Where to, lady?"

She could not hold back a smile. "How about our home?"

When they reached the house, the answering machine was blinking. Sylvia rushed to it and punched the button. A man from a florist shop was calling, and he sounded very much like the man who had called before, about the apricot roses. "Just wanted you to know, Mr. Benson, the lady loved the red roses. She said to tell you they were so beautiful they made her cry!"

Sylvia's blood ran cold. Randy may not have mentioned Chatalaine's name, but he was making sure she received flowers from him while he was away from her.

"Wow, am I ever glad to hear that," Randy said, moving up beside her. "I wanted those flowers to get to her as soon as possible. She needed to know someone cared about her."

Sylvia wanted to reach out and slap him. Hard. How dare he? When he had promised the week was to be hers?

"Poor Carol. I know she's hurting. No one ever sends her flowers. I hope those roses make her feel better."

Carol? He sent those flowers to Carol? Of course, he did! She's been his secretary for years. Sylvia nibbled on her lower lip, glad she had not blurted out something she would have regretted later. Feeling riddled with guilt, she picked up the phone and held it out to him. "You want to call the office?

See how things are going?"

He took it from her and placed it back in its cradle. "I'm sure things are fine." He looked about the room, his gaze fixing on the Venetian blind. "While I'm here, you want me to fix that window blind? I know it's been driving you crazy. I'm— I'm sorry I haven't gotten around to repairing it for you."

She nodded, grateful for his offer. The blind had been driving her nuts. Something in the mechanism was broken, and she had not been able to lower it to block out the late afternoon sun. "If you're sure you want to."

"Looks like I've got the time," he said with a grin, heading toward the garage, where he kept his tools.

She watched from her place on the sofa as he unfolded the stepladder and strapped on his tool belt, amazed at how handsome he was. *Women age. Men mature.* Where had she heard that silly saying? But it was true. Randy had matured, and on him, it looked good. No wonder that society columnist had gone after him.

"There you go. Good as new!" Randy crawled down and folded the ladder. "Go ahead. Give it a try."

Sylvia quickly moved to the window and gave a slight tug on the cords. As smooth as glass, the shade lowered into place. "Hey, thanks, that's great. Now the sofa won't fade."

"You're welcome. I'm just sorry I haven't done it before now. Got anything else that needs to be fixed?"

"The drain thingy in the lavatory in the half-bath off the kitchen won't lock down."

He gave her a mock salute before heading toward the little bathroom. "Tool-time Randy and his trusty tool belt are on their way!"

In ten minutes, he was back. "Why don't I check that filter in the furnace while I'm at it?"

For the rest of the afternoon, Randy made the rounds of

each room in the house, replacing lightbulbs, tightening screws, checking cabinet hinges and knobs, all sorts of manly me-fix-it projects. What impressed Sylvia most was the joy he seemed to get out of doing those things, the very things she had been at him for months to take care of.

By the time he finished, she had supper on the table.

"I knew it!" he said, coming into the kitchen after a quick shower. "Broccoli soup with garlic toast! I could smell it clear up in our bedroom!"

"I was hoping you'd be pleased." She checked the pot on the stove one more time and made sure the soup was not sticking to the bottom of the pan. "It's ready."

Randy rubbed his hands together. "Umm. Let me at it."

"You're not too full from those two hotdogs?"

He grinned. "What hotdogs?"

Again, Randy helped her clear the table and load the dishwasher when they had finished supper. Sylvia could not believe he had actually eaten two big bowls full of the broccoli soup and consumed four pieces of toast.

"What now?" he asked as they turned off the kitchen light and headed for the family room.

"I thought we'd watch a movie."

He wrinkled up his face. "Not a chick flick."

He headed for his recliner. She shook her head and pointed to the empty spot beside her on the green leather sofa. "Not there. Here."

He gave her a shy grin and settled himself down beside her while she punched the PLAY button on the remote control.

The tape began to roll, and Randy leaned forward, his eyes narrowed. "Naw, it can't be! An action movie? Surely not!"

Sylvia quirked a smile. "Don't tell me you've seen this one!"

He leaned back with a satisfied look. "Nope. I didn't even know it had been released to the video stores yet. I've been wanting to see it but—"

She rolled her eyes. "I know—you've been too busy."

"Exactly. But no more. From now on—I'm going to—"

"Take care of Number One," she inserted quickly, though it broke her heart to say it.

"Right! I didn't think you liked action movies," he said as the credits finished and the story started.

I hate them! "They're okay. Some of them have good story lines." *If you can weed them out from all the car chases and noise!*

Before long, Randy was so into the movie, he barely seemed to notice she was sitting beside him. *Will this thing ever end?*

When the movie ended, Randy took her hand in his and looked into her eyes. She held her breath; sure he was going to say something romantic.

"Is there any lemon meringue pie left?"

Men! She wanted to pick up one of the sofa pillows and pelt him like she had seen Shonna do to Buck, but instead she smiled sweetly. *Maybe the way to a man's heart is through his stomach after all. Hopefully, Chatalaine is a lousy cook!* "Sure. I'll cut you a piece."

Randy finished his piece of pie with an appreciative sigh. "That's the best pie I've ever tasted."

"Think you can sleep on a full stomach?" she asked him as she pointed to the clock on the fireplace. "It's after eleven."

He let out a big yawn, stretching his arms first one way, then the other. "Oh, yeah. I'm so tired I could sleep standing up. I can't believe how far we walked this morning."

They turned out the lights and made their way up the stairs to their room. This time, Randy did not question their sleeping arrangements. By the time Sylvia had washed her face and slipped into her gown, he was already sitting on his side of the bed in his pajamas. "Is that a new gown?"

She nodded. "Yes. Do you like it?" *I had it on last night.*

Were you so worried about sharing the bed with me you didn't even notice?

"Yeah, I like. What happened to those—"

"Granny gowns, as you used to call them? They're in the back of my closet. I'm thinking of giving them to Good Will. They're all cotton and would make wonderful rags," she added with a chuckle. "I'm making some changes in my life, too, Randy. Getting rid of my granny gowns and fuzzy slippers is one of them."

He gave her a quick once-over. "Well, you're a knockout in that gown. You should wear that color more often."

She moved across the bed on her knees and began her massage routine. Again, Randy did not protest. He just leaned over and let her willing fingers work on him again. "This has been a good day," he finally said when she moved back to her side of the bed. "Thank you for it."

"You're welcome." Giving him a playful grin, she slid under the covers and flipped onto her side, facing away from him, praising the Lord. Randy seemed mystified by her calmness, which is exactly what she wanted. "Good night, Randy."

"Good night, Syl."

nine

They awoke the next morning to another perfect Dallas day. After a hardy breakfast, they loaded into the car and headed for the zoo.

"Do you have any idea when I last visited a zoo?" Randy asked when they stopped at the gorilla section.

"I remember exactly. You were pushing DeeDee in her stroller, so I'd say that was about seventeen years ago. As I recall, you tilted that stroller up onto its rear wheels and jogged around the alligator pit, making motor sounds while she giggled and clapped her hands."

"Then, when she fell asleep, I carried Aaron on my shoulders while you pushed the stroller."

She threw her head back with a raucous laugh. "Poor little Buck! We made him wear that harness thing your mother bought so he wouldn't get lost. Remember how he hated that thing?"

"Do I! I finally had to take it off him. I couldn't stand his crying. Then he complained because we held onto both his hands."

"I guess—sometimes—we were overprotective."

"Hey, you!" Randy made a face at one of the gorillas, sticking his thumbs in his ears and wiggling his fingers at the animal.

Sylvia tugged on his arm. "Randy, people are staring at you!"

He shrugged complacently. "Who cares? Remember, I've turned over a new leaf! No more inhibitions!"

She eyed him with a shake of her head. *Turned over a new leaf? Sounds to me like the whole tree has fallen on your head!* "Oh, yeah. For a minute there, I forgot." She pointed to an area past

102

the gorilla section. "Look, there's the duck pond."

Randy bought a bag of feed from the little vending machine, and they sat down on a nearby bench, tossing the feed to the many ducks that gathered. "We sure had three cute kids, didn't we? It seems like only yesterday little DeeDee was letting the ducks eat out of her hand. Those were good times, Syl."

"Yes, they were. We didn't have much in the way of worldly goods, and at that time, neither of us knew Jesus, but we had each other and nothing else mattered." She let out a deep sigh. "How I wish we could go back to those sweet times."

Randy threw the remaining feed onto the ground, watching a dozen ducks scramble to snatch it up before the others got it. "But we can't, Syl. What's done is done, and there's no undoing it."

It could be undone, if you were willing to give it a try!

Randy suggested they stop by the sandwich shop near their house for lunch since Buck and Shonna would be coming for dinner in a few hours. By three, they were back home, with Sylvia tying an apron about Randy's waist so he could help her prepare dinner.

The minute Buck came through the door, Sylvia rushed into the living room and pulled him to one side, warning him to behave and not mention one word about the divorce or seeing his father with Chatalaine.

"How's it going?" Buck asked in a whisper.

"I'm not sure, but we've been getting along extremely well. He may be humoring me, but at least I'm having a chance to spend time with him—just the two of us—which we haven't done in a long time."

He doubled his fist and gave a playful blow to her chin. "Hang tough, Mom. Shonna and I are praying for you and Dad."

She stood on tiptoe and kissed his cheek. "I know, Buck. God is able. I'm counting on Him answering our prayers."

Randy came into the room, pulling off his apron. He cautiously extended his hand toward his son. With a huge grin, Buck took his hand and shook it heartily as his mother breathed a sigh of relief. The last thing she wanted was for her husband and son to have harsh words.

After greetings all around, the four moved into the dining room, where the candles were already burning brightly, to share the dinner Randy and Sylvia had prepared. The dinner conversation was light and cheery, with both Randy and Sylvia relating their experiences of the past two days. Everyone laughed when Sylvia told them about Randy making faces at the gorilla.

"You're lucky they didn't stick you in the cage with him," Shonna said with a giggle. "After a trick like that."

By ten, the couple left after much hugging and kissing. Randy lingered at the door until Buck's taillights disappeared into the darkness. "What a good guy our son has turned out to be."

"We can be very proud of our kids," Sylvia said, gathering up the empty glasses that had accumulated in the room and carrying them to the kitchen.

"So, what's on the agenda tomorrow? A trip to the local museum?" Randy asked as they climbed the stairs. "Are we going to check out the mummies or look at abstract paintings?"

"Neither. Tomorrow morning, I thought we'd stay home, but I have something planned for the afternoon. "

Randy stopped on the landing. "The whole morning at home? That sounds nice."

"But you have to make me a promise." She could see by his face that he expected a caveat. "I want you to call the office and make sure everything is going well."

He tilted his head quizzically. "You sure you want me to call? That wasn't part of the deal."

"It's my deal, which means I have the right to change the rules anytime I like," she said, pinching his arm playfully before turning and scurrying off to their room.

When she came out of the bathroom wearing another new nightgown, Randy noticed immediately and gave her a "Wow!" She did a quick turn around, twirling the long flowing skirt like DeeDee always did when she was a child playing dress-up in her mother's clothes.

Randy let out a long, low whistle. "I'd say getting rid of those granny gowns was a vast improvement!"

"You—you don't think it's too low cut? Too sheer?"

"No, ma'am. Not one bit!"

She crawled up onto the bed and pulled her Bible from the drawer. "If you don't mind, I thought I'd read a couple of chapters before going to bed."

He propped his pillow against the headboard and leaned against it. "Fine with me."

"That is, unless you're ready to go to sleep. I don't want the light to keep you awake." She gave him a coquettish smile again. "If you don't mind waiting a bit, I'll massage your neck muscles again. I noticed you rubbing at them when we were all sitting in the family room. Has your neck been bothering you, Randy?"

His hand rose and stroked at his neck. "Some. I asked a doctor about it. He said it was tension."

She put her Bible aside and crawled across the bed, moving up beside him, her hands kneading into the tight muscles. "You poor baby. Why didn't you tell me?"

"Nothing you could do about it. He said the only thing that would help was getting rid of some of the stress in my life, and that's not an easy thing to do."

Is that why you're trying to make such radical changes in your life? Because the doctor advised it? I'll bet he didn't tell you to get rid of your wife of twenty-five years. Did you tell him you had a girlfriend? "I'm sure it's not easy, with the job you hold at the paper."

"He said I'd better start getting more exercise, too. That long walk you and I took yesterday was just what the doctor ordered."

She worked his deltoids until her fingers began to cramp. After bending to kiss his cheek, she moved to her side of the bed and crawled under the quilt. "I'm really tired, and I know you are, too. Maybe we'd better put off reading the Bible until morning. Let's get some sleep. We have lots of work to do tomorrow."

Randy crawled into his side of the bed, propping himself up on his elbow. "Work? What kind of work?"

"You'll see." She gave him her sweetest smile before scooting to the edge of her side of the bed. "Good night, Randy."

"Good night, Syl." A second later, she heard the snap of the light switch, and the room fell into utter darkness.

"Syl?"

"Yes."

"Thanks for the neck rub."

"You're welcome."

"Syl?"

"Yes."

"Thanks for another great day."

"It was great, wasn't it?"

"Yeah. It was."

๛

Randy's eyes opened wide when the alarm sounded. Surely, it was not morning yet. He flinched! *Oh, oh! What am I doing?* His arm draped over Sylvia's shoulder, he was on her half of the bed. He froze when she moaned and reached toward her nightstand to turn off the alarm. He quickly withdrew his arm and scooted to his side, sitting up with a loud, exaggerated yawn. "What time is it?"

"Seven," she droned sleepily.

"Seven? I'm usually wide awake at five. You realize this week is going to throw my entire routine off whack, don't you?" He watched as she stood, reached her hands toward the ceiling with an all-out stretch, then headed toward the bathroom. *Boy, did I goof. I can't believe I was on her side of the bed after making such a big deal about sleeping in the guest room. But, wow! She looked so cute with that new haircut and wearing that fancy, low-cut red nightgown.* He shook his head to clear it. "Wanna tell me about today's project?" he called out to her.

She appeared in the bathroom doorway. "Not yet, but it'll be fun."

As he sat on his edge of the bed, waiting for her to return, his gaze fell to the Bible on her nightstand. How long had it been since he'd read his Bible? He shut his eyes tightly, trying to block out its vision. A shudder coursed through his body. *Are you sure you want to leave your wife?* a small voice seemed to ask from within his heart.

"I don't love her like I used to," he answered in a whisper.

You don't love her like you used to? Or are you turning your back on that love, trying to block it out to excuse your childish behavior?

Randy crossed his arms over his chest defiantly. "I've made up my mind. It is time for me now. For the past twenty-five years, I have sacrificed for my family, putting their needs first. I've worked round the clock to attain the position I have at the paper, spent every free hour I could find serving on the church board, and where has it all gotten me?"

You are in reasonably good health. You have a beautiful, loving wife, terrific kids, a great home, more than adequate income, and you are a born-again Christian. What more could you ask?

"Time for me! Time to do the things I'm interested in, before

I either die or simply cannot do them because of poor health or because I'm too old. There's so much I haven't experienced. When I come to the end of my life, I don't want to have regrets for the things I never did. Why can't people understand that?"

"Randy?"

His wife's voice brought him back to reality as she came out of the bathroom.

"Were you talking to someone? I heard voices."

"No, just talking out loud. Bad habit I seem to have picked up lately." He gave her a smile he hoped she did not perceive as guilt. "Among my other bad habits."

"See you downstairs," she said with a grin. "Gonna be a simple, quick breakfast this morning—juice, coffee, and cold cereal. We have things to do. Wear your jeans and a T-shirt."

Sylvia was already sitting at the kitchen table, sipping her juice when Randy arrived—showered, shaved, and ready for the day. Once the dishes had been loaded into the dishwasher, she reached for the two clean aprons hanging on a hook on the back of the pantry door. "One for me," she said, tying it about her waist, "and one for you."

"An apron? What's this for?"

"We're going to bake Christmas cookies!"

He gave her a skeptical stare, then allowed her to tie his apron about his waist. "This should be an experience!"

"It'll be fun, and remember, our kids will be home in a few days, and they'll be expecting homemade cookies. Think how proud you'll be when you tell them you helped me bake them!" She gave him a gentle swat on his seat. "Now go wash your hands. I'll get my cookbook."

He did as he was told, and by the time he was finished, Sylvia was already beginning to assemble the things they would need. "What kind are we going to make?"

She gave him a mischievous smile. "Actually, we're going to

make three kinds. Chocolate chip, of course, since all the kids—and you—love them. My famous spritz cookies run through the cookie press and decorated, and lastly, it wouldn't seem like Christmas without sugar cookies cut into all those wonderful shapes and sprinkled with red and green sugar crystals. So we'll have to make those, too."

"Wow, we are going to be busy." He rubbed his hands together briskly. Just hearing the names of the cookies made his mouth water. "What do you want me to do?"

She handed him a tall canister from the counter. "Take that big bowl and measure me out six cups of flour."

He placed the canister on the island, pulled a clean coffee cup from the cabinet, and began to measure out the flour. "Like this?"

Her eyes widened. "No, you can't use a coffee cup! You have to use a measuring cup!"

He gave her a shrug. "Why? A cup is a cup!"

"Oh, my, I can see I'm going to have to watch your every move."

Using the proper measuring cup, Randy began again to spoon out the flour. "Here you go," he said, trying to conceal a grin as he pushed the bowl toward her. "I lost count, but I think there are six cups in there."

Again her eyes widened.

"Just kidding, Syl, just kidding. There *are* six cups of flour in there. Honest."

She took the bowl from his hands and placed it on the counter next to the mixer. "I doubt it. It looks as though some of it went onto the floor, and you have to have at least a fourth of a cup on your apron!"

He looked quickly down at his apron, and she giggled aloud. "Just kidding, Randy. Gotcha!"

"What do you want me to do next?"

She motioned toward the kitchen wall phone. "Call your office."

He eyed her with a questioning smile. "Only if you want me to."

Fortunately, there were no major catastrophes going on at the office. A few minor ones, but the man he had left in charge was doing an admirable job of handling them. Randy was glad she had insisted he call. It set his mind at ease and made him realize it was only reasonable that he turn some of his responsibilities over to someone else. There was no way he could do it all.

They laughed their way through the three kinds of cookies, and by the time the last cookie sheet went into the oven, the kitchen was an absolute mess. Chocolate chips, red and green sugar sprinkles, and several colors of icing adorned the counters, the floor, and even the two cookie bakers, but the cookies looked beautiful spread out across the dining room table.

"I did it! I actually made cookies!" Randy said proudly as he stood beside Sylvia surveying their handiwork. He slipped an arm about her waist. "But I have to admit, babe, I never realized how much time and work you put into making all those Christmas cookies that seemed to appear by magic on Christmas Day. I don't think I ever thanked you."

❧

Sylvia blinked hard to hold back tears of gratitude as God's Word filled her heart, giving her renewed hope. *"Favour is deceitful, and beauty is vain; but a woman that feareth the Lord, she shall be praised. Give her of the fruit of her hands; and let her own works praise her in the gates."*

"Syl? Did you hear me?" Randy asked, giving her a slight squeeze.

"I—I heard you, Randy, but I want you to know—I never

expected any thanks. They were my gift to my beloved family. Yes, they took time and work, but I loved every minute of it. I made those cookies because I knew you and the children would enjoy them."

They had a quick bite of lunch, then worked side-by-side cleaning up the kitchen until it once again sparkled.

"You still haven't told me what we're going to do with the rest of the afternoon."

She tapped the tip of his nose with her finger. "You and I are going shopping!"

He responded with an unenthusiastic groan. "I hate shopping, you know that."

"You'll like this shopping. We're going to buy a Christmas tree!"

By the time they reached the third Christmas tree lot, Randy was a basket case, ready to accept any old tree, but Sylvia insisted they had to find just the right one.

"I know exactly what you want," the elderly man at the YMCA Christmas tree lot told them as she described the tree she had in mind.

Randy's excitement revived when he saw the tree the man selected for them. "It's perfect, Syl. It'll look great in the family room!"

She had to agree, it was perfect. The right kind, the right height, the branches were densely filled with needles, and the color was an exquisite, healthy dark green.

"We'll take it," Randy said enthusiastically, almost snatching the tree from the man's hands.

"Don't you want to ask how much it is first?" the ever-frugal Sylvia asked.

Randy shook his head vigorously. "I don't care what it costs. It's exactly what we were looking for!"

It was nearly four o'clock by the time they got the tree

mounted in the tree stand and placed in its majestic position in the corner of the family room. His hands on his hips, Randy stood back to admire it.

"Guess what you get to do!"

He turned to her with a frown. "Not the lights!"

She nodded. "Yes, the lights. Like you did on our first Christmas."

Together, they made several trips to the attic, bringing down all sorts of boxes and bags, until the entire family room floor was cluttered with decorations. As soon as they located the big box containing the lights, Randy began winding them around the tree, with Sylvia sorting out the various strings and handing them to him. Once the last string was connected and the extension cord in place, Randy proudly placed the plug in the wall and the beautiful tree came to life, with hundreds of tiny twinkling lights sparkling and blinking.

"Oh, Randy. It's beautiful! I've never seen a prettier tree. You did a great job with the lights."

His eyes surveyed the tree from top to bottom. "I kinda messed up there at the top. I should've put more lights up there."

She gazed at the tree, not caring if the lights were even. Randy had put those lights up—willingly. That is all that mattered. "I think it's perfect," she said dreamily.

He bent and kissed the top of her head. "You're biased."

For the next hour, they opened boxes, pulled out ornaments, and hung them on the tree. As they worked, they reminisced over each one, remembering where and when they had purchased them or who had given them to them as a gift. Some the children had made. Some Sylvia had made. Some others had made, but each one had its own special story.

"Remember when you bought me this one?" Sylvia asked, pulling a fragile, clear-glass angel from its fitted Styrofoam box.

He carefully took the ornament from her hand and stared at it. "Our tenth Christmas together?"

She nodded, surprised that he remembered. "Yes. You—you told me—"

"I—I told you that you were my angel. I bought it in the hotel gift shop when I was on a business trip to New York City. That face reminded me of you. You were supposed to come with me, but both DeeDee and Aaron came down with the chicken pox at the same time, and you had to stay home."

She felt her eyes grow misty. "I—I should've left them with my mother and gone with you. They would probably have been fine without me. Just like your office is getting along fine without you." She moved toward him, her hand cupping his arm. "Why didn't we find time for each other, Randy?"

He swallowed hard, then placed his free hand over hers. "I don't know. Life's demands, I guess."

Suddenly, he pulled away, and she was sure he did it to change the subject and break this melancholy mood they both seemed to be in. "Are—are you hungry?" she asked, wanting to put him back at ease. "I've got a pot of chili simmering on the stove."

His smile returned. "With grated fresh onion, cheese, and chips?"

"Just like you like it, and apple crisp for dessert."

After supper, when the kitchen had been restored to order, Sylvia led Randy back into the family room. "Tired?"

"A little. Stringing lights is hard work." He moved into his recliner and propped up the footrest, then sat staring at the tree. "Pretty, isn't it?"

"Absolutely beautiful! I've never seen a prettier tree." Sylvia punched the PLAY button on the CD player, and Christmas music filled the room.

"Me, either. It's nice just sitting here, watching the lights, listening to Christmas carols, and relaxing. Surely you don't have a project for tonight."

She smiled and shook her head. "Not really. I've already wrapped all the Christmas presents. I want to put them under the tree, that's all. You sit right there and watch me."

"You work too hard, Syl. I never realized how hard."

"Give her of the fruit of her hands; and let her own works praise her in the gates." "What I do isn't work, Randy. It's a labor of love." She bustled about the room and, after spreading around the base of the tree the Christmas skirt she had made several years ago, she pulled dozens of beautifully wrapped presents from the closet and arranged them on top of it. "There. All done."

He stared at the vast array of gifts. "When did you do all of that?"

"I started the week after Thanksgiving. Shopping for our family was like a—therapy—for me. It kept my mind off—things."

"I get the message," he said, leaning his head against the headrest. "I'm sorry, Syl, but there wasn't an easier way or a better time to tell you that I—"

She quickly pressed her fingers to his lips. "Shh. We're not going to talk about that this week. That was our agreement."

"I—I just don't want you to get your hopes up."

Though Sylvia remained silent, her mind was racing. *My hopes are up, Randy! I can't help it. However, I can see, if I am going to win you back, I'm going to have to give it everything I've got. Hopefully, what I have planned for tomorrow will bring you to your senses!*

ten

By the time Randy crawled out of bed the next morning, Sylvia had strung a long evergreen garland along the top of the mirror over the fireplace, arranged the fragile Nativity set on the dining room buffet, and placed dozens of Christmas decorations and Christmas candles all over the house. Many of them were things she herself had made over the years.

"Hey, why didn't you wake me up?" he asked, looking from one decoration to another. "I would've helped you."

She pointed to the empty boxes standing in the hall. "You can carry those boxes back up to the attic, if you want to help."

He grinned as he shoved up the short sleeve of his T-shirt and flexed his bicep. "Glad to. Easy task."

By ten, Sylvia was instructing Randy to pull the car into the parking lot of Dallas Memorial Hospital.

"Why here? I'm not sick, and you haven't mentioned feeling bad."

She smiled as she pushed her door open and climbed out. "Indulge me."

Once inside, they walked to the bank of elevators opposite the reception desk. As they entered the open one, Sylvia punched the button marked FIVE. She could feel Randy's eyes on her as the elevator ascended. She led him down a hall to a long set of plate glass windows with a sign above them that read NEWBORN NURSERY. "This look familiar?" The look on his face told her he well remembered the place.

❧

Randy pressed his cheek against the cool glass as memories

115

flooded his mind. "Oh, yes," he answered in a voice that sounded raspy, even to him. "Especially that little bed over there in the far corner. I thought we were going to lose him, Syl, and we nearly did." He felt her move up close to him and lean her head against his shoulder. "I'd never been so scared in all my life."

"The birth of a child is truly a miracle. God took the love of two young people who thought they had the world by the tail and, through their love, created a tiny image of the two of them and breathed the breath of life into him. Our little boy. Our precious first child. Our Buck."

Randy closed his eyes, his head touching hers, and tried to shut out the memory of the tiny baby as he had gasped for life with each tiny, laborious breath. "He—he was so small. So helpless. I could've held him in my palm."

"But God intervened and strengthened his little lungs. Our baby lived, and look at him now. Buck is tall, straight, and healthy. A real answer to prayer." She slipped her hand into the crook of his arm. "I can remember us both begging God to spare our child, making Him all sorts of promises. That was an emotional time for us, Randy, one I'll never forget. But there were happier times right here in this nursery, too. Remember when the twins were born?"

He rubbed at his eyes with his sleeve. "Do I ever! I was so afraid of losing you, I must've driven the doctors and nurses crazy. After the trouble we'd had with Buck, I couldn't imagine you giving birth to two babies!"

She snickered. "I was so worried about you, I had trouble concentrating on my breathing. I was afraid you were going to faint on me."

He wrapped his arm about her waist. "And I did! I was never so embarrassed in my life."

"You were only out a few seconds. Good thing that male

nurse caught you, or you might've ended up on the floor having to have stitches in your head."

"I'll never forget the experience of seeing our children born. How did you ever go through it, Syl? The pain must've been excruciating."

She leaned into him and gazed at the newborn in the little bed nearest the window. "Our babies were worth it." Watery eyes lifted to his. "They were *our* babies, Randy. Yours and mine. I loved them. I loved you."

For long moments, neither of them said a word, just continued to stare through the glass. Finally, Sylvia took his hand and silently led him back to the elevators. "There are several other things I want to show you," she said in a mere whisper as the elevator doors opened.

When they reached the corner of Fourth Avenue and Bogart, Sylvia instructed Randy to turn left.

"This looks very familiar. I think I know where we're headed. Are you sure this is a good idea, Syl?"

"Humor me, Randy, okay?"

He pulled through the cemetery gates, made a quick right turn, then a left, and parked at the side of the road. "Wanna reconsider?" he asked as she pushed open her door and made her way between the gravestones.

By the time she reached her destination, Randy was at her side. She knelt beside the tiny grave marked *Angela Renae Benson* and bowed her head. Seconds later, she felt Randy kneel beside her.

Sylvia tried to be brave, to keep her emotions under control, but she could not, and she began to weep.

"I'm sorry, Randy. Maybe you're right. Maybe coming here wasn't a good idea, but I wanted you to remember all the things we've gone through together. All the love and the joys and the heartaches we've shared."

"I—I do remember, Syl. I tried to be strong—for you—when we lost our little Angela, but inside I didn't feel strong. I felt like a failure. I wasn't even there for you when she was born. I was—too busy—at the newspaper, tending to some unimportant problem when you called and said your mother was taking you to the hospital. I should've dropped everything and rushed to your side, but I didn't."

She leaned against him, needing his strength. "It—it wasn't your fault, Randy. We would've lost her whether you made it or not."

"I—I wonder if she would've looked like DeeDee? With lots of dark curly hair and that cute little button nose?" He leaned forward and traced their baby's name with the tip of his finger.

"Angela was a product of our love, Randy, just like Buck and DeeDee and Aaron. She—she would've been ten years old in February."

"Let's go, Syl," he said tenderly as he rose and offered her his hand.

She stood slowly, giving the tiny grave one last look. Then she leaned into Randy as his arm encircled her, and they walked back to her car.

"Now where? Home?"

She pulled a tissue from her purse, blotted her eyes, then blew her nose loudly. "Not yet. Head on down Fourth Avenue and turn onto Lane Boulevard."

They rode silently for several miles, when suddenly Sylvia grabbed onto his arm and said, "Pull over."

"Oh, Syl. Not here!"

When he braked, she crawled out of the car and motioned for him to follow, carefully moving down a slight embankment toward a grove of trees. When she reached her destination, she stopped and turned to him. "I nearly lost you here,

Randy. I'll never forget that day."

He reached out and ran his fingers across a long diagonal scar on the nearest tree's trunk. "I thought for sure I was a goner when that drunk ran me off the road. It felt like I was doing ninety miles an hour when I left the boulevard, but I was only doing around forty according to the witnesses." He bent and rubbed at his knee. "I wasn't sure I was ever going to walk again."

"You could've been killed."

"I know."

"It was a miracle you lived. God spared you, Randy. He had a purpose for your life."

"I may never have walked again if it hadn't been for you and all those months of physical therapy you helped me with. How could you do it, Syl? With everything else you had to do, you put aside two hours a day to help me work my leg."

"Give her of the fruit of her hands, and let her own works praise her in the gates." "I wanted to do it, Randy. I loved you."

He took a couple of steps back, stuffing his hands into his pockets. "If you're trying to make me feel bad, you're succeeding."

"Making you feel bad is not my purpose, Randy. I just want you to remember the things that make up a marriage. Both good and bad."

He extended his hand, and they climbed back up the embankment. This time, Sylvia moved into the driver's seat.

They crossed town to an area near the college where Randy had attended school and obtained his degree in journalism. Sylvia brought the car to a stop in front of a rundown old tenement building.

Randy shielded his eyes from the sun as he stared at the place they had once lived, pointing up to the third floor with his free hand. "That was our apartment right up there. I can remember you standing in that very window, smiling and waving at me when I came home from class every afternoon."

"Seeing you coming up that sidewalk was the highlight of my day. What fun we had," Sylvia said, waxing nostalgic. "Remember those old wooden crates you got out of the dumpster at some warehouse. We used those for end tables and a coffee table and thought they were grand. I don't remember who gave us that old brown frieze sofa bed, but it did the job. I loved that apartment. Our very first home. I was so proud of it."

He laughed, and his laughter made her smile. "You were easy to please." His smile disappeared. "I always hated it that you had to work nights to put me through school. As I sat in that apartment each night, studying, I kept thinking about you waiting tables in that all-night restaurant and the creeps that must've come in there. I should never have let you support me like that, and you sacrificed your own education to make sure I got mine."

"But you sacrificed, too! You cared for Buck while you were studying. Otherwise, I couldn't have worked. We sure couldn't afford a baby-sitter, and neither of us wanted to leave him with one anyway." She gave his arm a reassuring pat. "I didn't mind. Honest."

His fist pounded into the palm of his other hand. "That place was a dump! I can't believe we lived there."

"That *dump* was an answer to prayer, Randy. Remember how excited we were when we finally found something we could afford?"

"I remember promising you we'd be out of there and in a better place in a year. We ended up staying there nearly all four years!"

"Just knowing you wanted a better place for us and were working to get your education so we could eventually have one was enough for me." She grabbed onto his hand and tugged him to the little drugstore on the corner. Once inside, she went to the soda fountain and ordered two root beers, a delicacy they had only been able to afford when she had worked a little overtime at the restaurant or some customer had left an overly generous tip. They sat side-by-side on the tall soda fountain stools and sipped their drinks the way they had done it nearly twenty-five years ago. On the way out, Sylvia bought a bag of red licorice, the long, stringy kind, another delicacy they had indulged in from time to time. She opened the bag and handed several strings to Randy.

He bit off a long piece, then winced. "We actually liked this stuff?"

She gave him a wink. "Come on—you loved it and you know it!"

He grinned. "Yeah, I guess I did."

"Beat you to the car," she hollered over her shoulder as she took off down the block. He did not catch up with her until she had reached the car.

He threw his arms around her as they both stood leaning against the car, panting and breathless. "What are you trying to do, lady? Throw me into a heart attack? I haven't run like that since—since—"

She chucked him under the chin with a giggle. "Oh? It's been so long you can't even remember when?"

"Maybe!" He pulled open the passenger door. "Who's driving? Me or you?"

"I'll drive." She crawled in, started the car, and waited until he had his seatbelt fastened. "One more stop, then we can go home."

She only had to drive a few blocks to reach their final destination for the day—a little red brick church on a crowded lot, surrounded by a tall wrought-iron fence. She expected Randy to protest, but when he did not, she opened the door and climbed out. As she had hoped, the big wooden doors were standing open. Slowly, she walked inside, hoping Randy would follow.

An elderly woman who was waxing the pews smiled up at her as she entered. Without a look back to see if Randy was behind her, she moved slowly to the altar and knelt on the worn kneeling pads, folding her hands in prayer.

When she finished praying and looked up, she found Randy kneeling beside her. "This is the exact spot where we gave our hearts to the Lord, Randy. Do you remember?" she whispered.

He nodded.

"Though we used to attend church here occasionally, until that morning, neither of us had much interest in the things of the Lord, but when the pastor brought that message—"

"About engraving us on the palms of his hands and how God has a plan for each of us, a plan to prosper us and not harm us?"

Sylvia turned to him in amazement. "You do remember!"

"Isaiah 49:16 and Jeremiah 29:11. I'll never forget those verses. They've helped me through some hard times."

Tears pooled in her eyes, making it difficult to see his face. "Hard times, like now?"

Randy stared into her eyes for a moment, and though she could not be sure, she almost thought she saw traces of remorse. But he turned away and walked back up the aisle, leaving her alone at the altar. She quickly bowed her head once more and poured out her heart to God. "Lord Jesus, only You can put this family back together again. Please soften Randy's heart, and God, make me be the kind of wife You would have me be. I so want to serve You. I want to know that perfect plan You have for me and for Randy.

Forgive me for the many times I've sinned against You. Only now, since Randy has been back home and I've examined my own life, have I seen how I, too, have been responsible for the problems we're facing. Help me to do Your will. Please, God, please!"

They stopped at Randy's favorite steak house for dinner and, although steak was not Sylvia's favorite, she ordered the same thing Randy ordered and willed herself to enjoy it. When Randy excused himself to go to the men's room, Sylvia held her breath, hoping he was not going to phone Chatalaine. Funny he had not mentioned her name, not once since he had arrived on the nineteenth. But why should he? No doubt he knew even the mention of her name would start an argument. No, Randy was too savvy for that. As long as she did not mention the woman's name, she was sure he would not, either. However, he was back in no time. No way would he have had time to phone the woman.

When they reached home, Randy plugged in the Christmas lights while Sylvia cued up another Christmas CD. They stayed up long enough to watch the nightly news and one of the late night talk shows before heading upstairs.

"Big day tomorrow," she told him as she climbed into bed. "The kids will be here for Christmas Eve, and we—you and I— have gobs of food to prepare. DeeDee and Aaron promised to be home by four, and Buck and Shonna are coming as soon as he gets off work."

Randy set the alarm on his side of the bed and flipped off the light before sliding under the covers. "Syl?"

"Yes."

"I can't say I exactly enjoyed today, but I have to admit it was an eye-opener."

"Oh?"

"I mean—I'd almost forgotten some of the things you and

I have gone through together. I guess I—put them out of my mind."

"That's understandable. I wanted to forget some of them, too."

"Syl?"

"Yes."

"I don't want you to get the idea that I'm hard-hearted, but at the same time, I don't want you to get your hopes up. I'm still planning on going through with the divorce."

"Good night, Randy. I love you."

Silence.

Suddenly, she felt Randy's weight shift in the bed, then his warm body snuggle up next to hers, his arm draping over her. "Good night, Syl."

Her heart pounded so furiously, she was sure he could feel the vibration. "Good night, Randy. Sleep tight."

Sylvia jerked out of Randy's arms and sat up with a jolt as his alarm sounded at seven. *Today is December the twenty-fourth! I have less than forty-eight hours to convince Randy to forget about the divorce and move back home where he belongs! Help, Lord!*

"Why don't I fix breakfast today?" Randy asked as he crawled out from under the covers and stretched his long arms.

Sylvia glanced at the Bible on her nightstand. "You sure you don't mind?"

"Not a bit! I'll come back up and take a shower later. Just don't expect anything too fancy."

She waited until she heard him go down the stairs, then picked up her Bible and began to read. *I'm sorry, Lord. Although it seems I keep shooting prayers up at You continually, I've neglected my Bible reading since Randy has come back home.* She turned to one of her favorite chapters, Psalm 139, and began to read. "O, Lord, thou hast searched me, and known me. Thou knowest my downsitting and mine uprising, thou understandest my thought afar off." She read through the few verses silently until she came to the twenty-third verse. "Search me, O God, and know my heart: try me, and know my thoughts: And see if there be any wicked way in me, and lead me in the way everlasting." *That's my prayer, Lord. Please, show me how to make these last few hours count. I can't lose my husband!*

As Sylvia reached for her jeans, she thought she heard the front door close. But deciding the noise must have been Randy working down in the kitchen, she went into the bathroom to put on her makeup and fix her hair. By the time she reached the kitchen twenty minutes later, he was sitting at the table waiting for her, a large white sack resting in the center.

"How does an Egg McMuffin sound?"

"Wonderful," she responded happily, meaning it, as she sat down beside him and reached for the sack.

❧

The strains of "Silent Night" filled the house as the six members of the Benson family gathered around the dining room table. Randy, Sylvia, Buck, Shonna, DeeDee, and Aaron. Sylvia's heart was so filled with gratefulness that they were all together like this—this one more time—she thought it would burst. Her wonderful son, knowing the secret their parents were carrying and apparently wanting to take the strain off his father and mother, offered to say the blessing on their food. Sylvia had hoped Randy would insist on doing it. However, when he kept his silence, she gave Buck an appreciative smile and a nod, and they all reached for one another's hands, forming a circle. Buck's prayer was brief but sincere, as he asked God to bless the food and the hands that prepared it and to bless each one assembled, especially his mom and dad.

"Your dad has been helping me all day," Sylvia told her family as she passed the carving knife to her husband.

Aaron gave a teasing snort. "Hey, Dad, why've you been

hiding your culinary talents all these years? This stuff looks pretty good!"

DeeDee slapped playfully at her twin brother. "Be quiet, Aaron, or he may never do it again."

"Tell me what you fixed, Dad, so I can avoid it," Aaron added, backing away from DeeDee as she swung at him again.

"I'm not telling," Randy said with a chuckle as he began to slice off thick wedges of the roasted turkey. "You'll either have to take your chances or starve. Your choice."

Aaron cocked his head as he weighed his options. "You win. I'll take my chances. Pass the mashed potatoes."

"I think everything looks wonderful, Father Benson," Shonna said as she held out her plate. "You and Mother Benson make a great team."

Sylvia gave her an exaggerated bow. "Thanks, Shonna. It's nice to be appreciated."

"We all appreciate you, Mom," Buck interjected with a quick sideways glance toward his father. "Don't we, Dad?"

"We sure do. I'm just beginning to realize all your mother does for this family. Giving us great meals like this is just a small part of it."

Sylvia's heart pounded erratically. "Thank you, Randy. It was—was sweet of you to say that." *"Give her of the fruit of her hands; and let her own works praise her in the gates."*

"Hey, are you going to give me a piece of that turkey, Dad," Aaron asked with a playful frown, "or am I going to have to arm wrestle you for it?"

The meal continued pleasantly with good-humored bantering going on between Randy and his sons.

After the last bite had been consumed and everyone's napkin returned to the table, Shonna and DeeDee volunteered to clear the table and help Sylvia clean up the kitchen, suggesting the men go into the family room and relax. Once everything was back in shape and the dishwasher humming away, the women joined them. Buck was already at the piano playing a Christmas carol.

"Hey, all of you," he told the gang, gesturing for them to join him, "it's time for the Benson family sing-along."

The five gathered around him and joined in as he led off with "O Holy Night." Sylvia's breath caught in her throat as Randy moved next to her, harmonizing with her as they had done so many times before. They sang three more carols, then Aaron suggested it was time for their annual reading of the Christmas story from the second chapter of Luke before they turned to the opening of the presents.

"Why don't you read this year, Buck?" Randy said, reaching for the big family Bible on the bookshelf. "My throat is a bit husky."

As her son gave his father a frown, Sylvia felt her mouth go dry. *Don't say anything you'll be sorry for, Buck. Please!*

Buck reached out and took the Bible from his hands without comment and opened it to Luke 2 and, after allowing everyone time to be seated, began to read.

"I love that chapter," DeeDee said as her older brother closed the Bible and returned it to its place. "You helped me memorize it when I was a kid, Dad. Remember? The first year I was on the church quiz team."

All eyes went to Randy. "Yeah, I guess I did. You were a quick learner, as I recall."

"Just think," Aaron said, dropping down on the floor near the tree and drawing his knees up to his chest, circling them with his arms, "God sent His only Son to earth as a baby, knowing He would die on the cross to save us from our sins. Isn't that an awesome thought?"

Sylvia moved to the leather sofa and settled herself beside her daughter-in-law. "It's hard to fathom He could love us that much, when we're so unworthy."

"What do you think of the tree your mother and I picked out and decorated?"

All eyes turned to Randy as he abruptly changed the subject. "Pretty, huh? I put the lights on."

"It's beautiful, Daddy," DeeDee said, leaning over her father to kiss his cheek. "You did a good job."

"I didn't know the old man had it in him," Aaron chimed in with a wink. "How come Mom's had to decorate the tree by herself all these years?"

"I—I like decorating the tree," Sylvia inserted quickly, not wanting Randy to have to explain himself. "But it was nice to have your dad do it for a change."

"Whose turn is it to distribute the presents this year?" Aaron picked up the gift nearest him and gave it a shake. "Looks like the man in the red suit has already been here and gone."

Sylvia leaned forward and swatted at him. "Don't talk that way, Aaron. I've always thought talking about Santa and pretending he's the one who brings the presents takes the glory away from Jesus and the real meaning of Christmas."

Aaron did an exaggerated double take. "You mean there really isn't a Santa Claus?"

"Just for that remark, young man, you can pass out the gifts," Sylvia said, hoping this wouldn't be the last Christmas her family would all be gathered like this. She could not imagine Christmas without Randy sitting in his chair.

"Okay, if you insist." Aaron began picking up the presents, reading the name on each tag out loudly, shaking the package, and predicting what he thought might be inside before handing it to the person for whom it was intended.

"Here you go, DeeDee. I'm guessing Buck and Shonna are giving you—a Barbie doll!"

He turned to his older brother. "Buck, inside this present DeeDee is giving to you, I predict you have a—a—a teddy bear!"

Randy's present came next. "Wow, Dad, what do you suppose is in this little box from Mom? Maybe that new set of golf clubs you told me you wanted?"

Sylvia watched with expectation as Randy opened her present.

"Oh, Syl," he said as he tore the last bit of paper off and opened the box. "You shouldn't have."

"What is it, Dad?" DeeDee asked, sliding closer to his chair.

"It's—it's the palm-sized video camera I've been wanting. How did you know—"

Sylvia grinned. "Buck told me you'd mentioned it to him. I hope I got the right one. You can exchange it if—"

"It's exactly the one I wanted. Thanks, Syl. Now I can take pictures of this motley crew as they open the rest of their presents."

Sylvia breathed a contented sigh. He liked her gift.

On and on and on it went, with each of Aaron's gift predictions sending the group into fits of laughter. Sylvia wanted to remember those sounds forever. As she glanced at the clock, she felt panic set in. Only twenty-eight hours to go, and although she and Randy had experienced some wonderful times since he'd arrived on the nineteenth, he seemed no closer to changing his mind about staying than when he'd arrived.

"And this last one is for Dad," Aaron said as he stood and hand-delivered it to his father. "Another one from Mom. How many does that make? Looks like you came out better than the rest of us this year."

"That's not true. Each of you—"

Aaron held up a finger and waggled it at his mother. "Just kidding, Mom. Don't get bent out of shape. After all, that old man is your husband. He'll be around long after us kids move out for good."

Randy sent her a quick glance that chilled her bones.

"Well, that's it!" Aaron reached for the big trash bag Sylvia had brought in to hold all the torn wrapping paper and ribbons.

She looked down at the presents piled on the coffee table in front of her. Each of the children had given her wonderful gifts, and she was grateful for each one of them, but none of the gifts had been from Randy, and she wanted to break down in tears.

"Actually," Buck said, rising and taking Shonna's hand in his, "there's another present coming, but it won't be delivered for some time. Shonna and I are going to have a baby! In July!"

Sylvia's heart leaped for joy. How she had longed to have a grandchild to cuddle and care for. She was going to be a grandmother! Her gaze went to Randy, who was just sitting there, as if in a stupor.

"Hey, old man!" Aaron said, punching his father in the arm. "You're gonna be a grandpa!"

Randy donned a quick grin and stood as both Buck and Shonna hurried to his side. "Congratulations, son. You, too, Shonna. That's gonna be one lucky baby. You two will make great parents."

"Aw, they won't be half as good as you and Mom," Aaron said, hugging his mother's neck.

"Who wants dessert?" Randy asked as he surveyed the group. "Your mom and I made her famous Millionaire Pie."

Buck raised his hand. "I'll take a very small piece. I'm stuffed with those fabulous Christmas cookies you and Mom baked. Those things are good!"

"Thank you, thank you, thank you!" Randy bowed low, then asked, "Small pieces of pie for everyone?"

The entire group shouted yes in unison.

"I'll help Dad," Buck said, motioning Sylvia to remain seated.

A cry choked in her throat. *Buck, no! Please don't say anything to your dad about Chatalaine or the divorce. Or about him not giving me a gift. Please!* She watched in fear as the two men headed for the kitchen.

Seeming to sense her fear, Shonna slid over on the sofa and wrapped her arm about Sylvia's shoulder. "It'll be okay. Buck won't say anything," she whispered so only her mother-in-law could hear.

A few minutes later, Buck and Randy came back into the room carrying six plates with small wedges of pie on them. Buck passed out the plates while Randy handed each person a fork and napkin.

As Sylvia started to rise again, Buck shook his head. "I'll get the coffee and cups, Mom. You eat your pie."

She gave him a slight grin, thankful for his thoughtfulness.

"Buck and I had quite a talk in the kitchen," Randy told everyone as he forked up his first bite of pie.

Sylvia nearly choked.

"He tells me he's thinking about going back to college for his master's."

"I think he should," Aaron said, nodding. "He's a smart guy."

They continued with good conversation until, eventually, the pie was gone. "I have to get up early, Mother Benson, so we'd better be going. We're due at my parents' house at ten, and I still have to make two pies tonight."

"You are going to be here for breakfast, aren't you?" Sylvia asked quickly.

Buck bent and kissed his mother's cheek. "Sure, Mom.

We'll be here by eight. We wouldn't miss your famous cinnamon rolls."

Aaron rose and tugged his sister to her feet. "We'd better get to work, too, little sister."

"Work? You two?" Buck asked with a teasing smile.

Aaron nodded. "Yep. Our friends are picking me and DeeDee up at ten for our ten-day skiing trip to Colorado, and we haven't even started packing our gear."

DeeDee took her mother's hand and patted it with concern. "You and Dad going to be okay? Being here by yourselves on Christmas Day?"

Sylvia nodded. "We'll be fine, honey. Just enjoy yourselves. I know you two have been looking forward to this ski trip since last year. Just promise me you'll be careful."

Everyone walked Buck and Shonna to the door. After hugs all around and more congratulations to the expectant parents, the couple left, and Randy closed the door.

Aaron and DeeDee each kissed their parents, thanked them for a wonderful Christmas, and headed up the stairs to their rooms.

"I—I think I'll go to bed, too," Sylvia said, as she gathered up her gifts. With a heavy heart, she climbed the stairs, leaving Randy to turn off the lights and check the doors, a job she had taken over in his absence.

I have to forget my husband didn't even give me a present. I can't let him see me sulking like this. Maybe, since he's spent the week with me, he simply didn't have a chance to do any shopping. I have to stop feeling sorry for myself. Deciding a quick shower might lift her spirits, she gathered up her gown and slippers and moved into the bathroom. When she came back out fifteen minutes later, Randy was sitting on the side of the bed in his pajamas, reading the instructions for his new video camera.

Sylvia pasted on her cheeriest smile as she sashayed across

the room toward him. *If Randy does leave, I want him to remember me smiling and looking radiant and more like the woman he married twenty-five years ago.*

He looked up with a broad smile, as if nothing whatsoever was wrong. "Hey, another new gown? I really like this one! Even better than the red one."

She twirled around, holding her hands out daintily like a ballerina, and ended up sitting on the bed beside him.

"Oh, I like that perfume!"

She lifted her head, offering her neck to him. He bent and took in an exaggerated whiff. "Zowie! Now that's what I call a perfume!"

She gave him a coy smile. "You bought it for me for Christmas two years ago."

"Do I have good taste, or what?"

"Thanks for another wonderful day, Randy," she said as she crawled onto the bed beside him, her fingers cupping his neck. "I think the kids had a good time tonight. I know I did." She began to knead his muscles as he tilted his head to one side. "That was some present Buck and Shonna gave all of us. Can you believe we're going to be grandparents?"

"I always wondered what it would be like to hold my first grandchild in my arms. I guess we'll find out in July."

She loved touching his skin, wafting in his manly scent, feeling his hot breath on her hands. She longed to leap into his lap and smother him with kisses, but if she did, she knew he'd probably run for the door, and she wouldn't have that one last day with him, so she restrained herself.

"There, does that feel better?" She scooted off the bed and bent to kiss his cheek. Suddenly, Randy grabbed her and pulled her to him, kissing her more passionately than he had done in years. Although surprised by his sudden action, she melted into his arms, fully participating in their kiss.

"You are so beautiful," Randy whispered in her ear as he held her close and nuzzled his face in her hair. "I've missed the closeness we used to share." He kissed her again, holding her in his arms tighter than ever.

"I've missed it, too," she whimpered breathlessly against his lips.

"This has been one of the best weeks of my life, Syl. I'll never forget it."

She clung to him, wishing this moment could last forever, but just as quickly as he had pulled her to him, he pushed her away.

"Hold me, Randy! Please! I love you!"

"I—I can't! Don't you see? I'll be leaving tomorrow night! Holding you and kissing you like this—well, it isn't fair to either of us. Our marriage is over, Syl! It died a long time ago! What we're having this week is make-believe."

She could not believe what she was hearing! She had been so sure God was answering prayer. "But, Randy, you said this was one of the most wonderful weeks of your life! We've had a great time together! We're going to be grandparents!"

"You don't get it, do you, Syl? Just because we've both been bitten by the festivities and hoopla of Christmas doesn't mean things won't return to what they were before when we get back to normal. We've both been like Ken and Barbie this past week! On our best behavior. Working to please each other and avoiding having words. We've been blinded by the joys and frivolity of the Christmas season. Bright lights, candles, ornaments, music. What happens when Christmas is over and the lights and ornaments are put back in their cardboard boxes and returned to that drab attic? I can't take that chance. It took me nearly two years to get up the courage to tell you how I really felt—how unhappy I've been. I can't go through it again!"

She wanted to slap him, scream, hit a door, something,

anything to wake him up. "Can't you see I love you, Randy? This hasn't all been your fault. I see that now! However, we can both change. We can work out our problems and differences if we really want to do it. We can't throw this marriage away like last week's copy of your newspaper. Our marriage is a living and growing thing!"

"A living thing that has been dying a slow death, Syl. It's time for the burial." He snatched up his pajamas and headed toward the bathroom, closing the door behind him.

Sylvia had never felt so hurt and rejected. Why hadn't she seen this coming? How blind and stupid could she have been? With tears flowing, she climbed into bed and pulled the sheet over her head. She heard Randy come out of the bathroom, felt him crawl into bed, and heard the click of the lamp.

Twenty-four hours. If I can't convince Randy to stay by then, it's all over. I promised I'd let him have the divorce, and I have to keep my word. Father God, are You listening, or are You forsaking me, too?

"Syl?"

She wanted to pretend she was asleep, but she could not. "Yes."

"Good night."

"Good night, Randy."

Sylvia lay awake until the red numbers on the clock showed 3:00 a.m. From the even rhythm of Randy's breathing, she was sure he was asleep, though she herself had barely closed her eyes. She crawled carefully out of bed and padded gently down the stairs, mumbling to herself. "Someone has to put the stockings up and fill them with little gifts and candy. Since Santa isn't real, I guess I'll have to do it."

"Give her of the fruit of her hands; and let her own works praise her in the gates."

eleven

December 25 dawned even more beautiful than any other day in the week they had been together. Although Sylvia was dead tired from lack of sleep, she jumped out of bed with a smile. *This is your last chance, girl. Make the most of it!*

Randy turned over with a frown. "You're chipper this morning."

"Why shouldn't I be? It's Christmas morning, and my family will all be gathered around the table for breakfast." She snapped her fingers, then yanked the cover off him. "Rise and shine, Grandpa!"

He covered his face with his hands. "Grandpa? That term sounded nice last night, but this morning, just the mention of it makes me feel old."

She crossed the room and opened the blinds, letting the room fill with sunshine. "Not me! It makes me feel young. I can hardly wait for the patter of little feet in this house again."

He pulled himself to a sitting position and ran his fingers through his hair. "Are you forgetting dirty diapers?"

"I don't even mind those." She poked him in the ribs with the tips of her finger. "Hustle, hustle! Buck and Shonna will be here soon. You don't want them to see you in those hideous pajamas, do you?"

He looked down at his pajamas. "What's wrong with them?"

"The colors are nice, but have you looked closely at the pattern?"

He raised an arm and squinted at the sleeve. "No."

"Randy! Those yellow dots are little ducks!"

"Ducks? I thought they were polka dots. Why didn't you tell me? I was in such a hurry when I bought them, I guess I never really looked at them."

"No, I'm sorry to tell you, but those are not polka dots; those are ducks. Cute little yellow duckies." She hurried to the door. "The kids will be here in ten minutes. If you don't want them to tease you about your ducks, you'd better get dressed."

"Is that another new T-shirt?" he called after her. "Looks good on you. I like purple!"

She had to smile. "Yes," she called back over her shoulder. "I bought it because I thought you'd like it!"

By the time she had filled the coffeepot and put the rolls in the oven, the front door opened and Buck and Shonna came bustling in. Within seconds, DeeDee and Aaron came down the stairs, with Randy two steps behind them. "Well," she said with a joy that overwhelmed her sorrow, "looks like the gang's all here. Anyone want to check their stockings?"

Buck, Shonna, DeeDee, Aaron, and even Randy, all made a mad dash to the family room, pulling their stockings from the fireplace and rummaging through their contents, pulling out the little wrapped gifts, whistles, paper hats, balloons, bubblegum, trinkets, and candy canes. Randy put on his paper hat, looped two candy canes over his ears, and paraded through the room loudly blowing his whistle while the whole family laughed hysterically. Buck soon joined him, followed by Shonna, DeeDee, and Aaron. Sylvia could stand it no longer, pulled on her hat, draped her candy canes over her ears, and stuck a whistle in her mouth, too. Following Randy's lead, the little battalion made their way through the house, traipsing through nearly every room, until they were all too weak with laughter to keep it up any longer.

"Now that we've made complete fools of ourselves," Sylvia

said, pulling the candy canes from her ears, "does anyone want breakfast?"

The Benson family laughed their way through breakfast, enjoying the huge platter of homemade cinnamon rolls Sylvia had baked, along with juice, coffee, and the large slices of the country ham she'd put in a slow oven when she'd gotten up to fill the stockings.

Buck and Shonna left at nine thirty to go to her parents' house. At ten, DeeDee and Aaron kissed their parents goodbye and joined the group of eager skiers honking in their driveway. Sylvia cast a cautious glance at the clock. *Fourteen hours to go.*

As soon as the door closed behind them, Randy tugged on her hand. "Come on, Grandma. I'll help you clean up the breakfast mess."

Putting on the best smile she could muster, she followed him into the kitchen and began gathering the dirty dishes and carrying them to the sink while he put things in the refrigerator. *I've got to stop counting the hours!*

"You outdid yourself again. These cinnamon rolls are the best you've ever made." He unwound a rounded section of the last roll on the plate, broke it off, and popped it into his mouth.

"Thanks. I'm glad you enjoyed them."

"So, what's the plan for today?" He slipped the empty plate into the dishwasher, then placed a hand on her wrist with a winning smile. "By the way, Merry Christmas."

She reached up and planted a quick kiss on his cheek. "Merry Christmas to you, too, Grandpa." *Why didn't you get me a present, Randy? Am I that unimportant to you? Do you hate me that much? I'll bet you got your little cutie a wonderful present!* "And by the way, we're staying home. All day."

"I was hoping you'd say that."

Once the kitchen was cleaned up, Sylvia pulled a covered dish from the freezer and left it on the counter to thaw for lunch. Then the two of them headed for the family room. To her surprise, Randy plunked himself down on the sofa instead of moving to his recliner. She picked up the copy of the *Dallas Times* that Buck had brought in when he and Shonna had come for breakfast and sat down beside Randy. "I put on a fresh pot of coffee," she said trying to sound casual as she pulled the oversized Christmas Day paper from its wrapper. She shuffled through the various sections, finally coming to the sports section, which she handed to Randy. As soon as his attention was focused on it, she quickly pulled out the "Dallas Life" section, bearing that spectacular picture of Chatalaine and her willowy figure and Cheshire cat smile, folded it, and placed it on the lamp table on her side of the sofa, face down. Compared to that woman, Sylvia felt dowdy, rumpled, and old. As soon as she had a chance, she planned on putting it in the trash container. No need for Randy to be reminded of his paramour on this, her final day with him.

Randy scanned through the sports section, then placed it on the coffee table. "Not much sports news today." He gazed at her for a moment, then cautiously slipped an arm about her shoulders and pulled her close. "I want you to know, Syl, how much I appreciate everything you've done to make this Christmas special for all of us. The kids, me." He hesitated as he raised a dark brow. "I—I hope we can always remain friends—for our children's sake."

Her heart dropped to the pit of her stomach, and she swallowed both her pride and a hasty reply. *Hold your anger! You have less than thirteen hours left. Don't blow it! Make every minute count. This may be your last chance to woo him back.* Instead of snapping his head off, which was what she would have liked to do, she smiled up at him, cradling his freshly shaven cheek with her hand. "Can we put this conversation off until later? I don't want to even think about it now."

He gave her a puzzled look, apparently caught off-guard by her unexpected response. "Ah—yeah—I just wanted to make sure you—"

Deciding to make her move, since she really had nothing more to lose, she whirled about and climbed onto his lap and began to stroke his hair, her face mere inches from his. Though he eyed her suspiciously, he did not move. After giving him an adoring smile, she tenderly kissed first one eyelid, then the other. One cheek, then the other cheek. Slowly, she let her lips move to his mouth, his closeness playing havoc with her senses. "I love you, Randy. You may leave me, but you'll never be able to forget me," she murmured softly as her mouth sought his again. She nearly screamed out as his arms circled her, pulling her against him. *Please, Randy, say you love me, too!*

When their kiss ended, she rested her forehead against his, her fingers twined about his neck. "Don't do it, sweetheart, don't leave me. We have so much for which to be thankful. Some of our best years are yet to come. Don't let them get away from us."

As if her words suddenly brought him back to reality, back to his unshakable resolve, he pushed her away and turned his head. "Don't, Syl, don't do this!" Literally picking her up and setting her off his lap onto the sofa, he stood to his feet, clenching and unclenching his fists at his sides.

Tears of humiliation and hurt stung at her eyes as she struggled to meet his icy glare. "But, Randy—"

"Is there any coffee left? I need a cup."

She drew a quick breath through chalky lips. Brushing her tears aside, she stood, her heart thundering, and hurried toward the kitchen. "I think we both could use a good, strong cup of coffee. I'll get it."

Once in the kitchen, she worked frantically to pull herself together, dabbing at her eyes with a dish towel and mulling over what had just happened. *Come on, Sylvia, get hold of yourself. Maybe you moved too fast, too aggressively; after all, that's not your style. You probably frightened him.* She gave a snort. *And that Chatalaine woman wasn't aggressive? If not, how did she manage to snare my husband away from me so easily and so quickly? She was probably all over him. Telling him how handsome he was. How smart. How successful—batting her baby blues at him.* She filled their coffee mugs, lifted her chin, and moved back into the family room, determined to keep Randy from seeing how badly his words had hurt her. "Here ya go! Strong, just like you requested."

She watched as Randy took the cup and seated himself on the floor in front of the sofa, sticking his long legs out in front of him. "Mind if I sit down beside you?"

"Of course not."

She sat down, crossing her legs at the ankles and took a long, slow sip of her coffee, hoping the tension between them was surmountable. Suddenly, she noticed a Christmas CD was playing. Randy must have turned it on while she was in the kitchen. "I love that CD."

He leaned back against the sofa and tilted his head as if listening to the song with rapt attention. "Folks should play Christmas carols all year. Seems a shame to play them only in December."

"I think I could sit here forever, watching the lights blink on the tree and listening to that music." She made a nervous gesture to brush her hair away from her face.

They sat silently until the CD finished playing, then picking up their empty mugs, Sylvia rose. "I—I guess I'd better get us some lunch."

"Need any help?"

She shook her head. "Thanks, but no. I'll bring our trays in here." Fifteen minutes later, she returned, handing Randy his tray as he moved up onto the sofa.

"Umm, your barbecue ribs? I hoped that was what I smelled."

"And the mustard potato salad you always liked to go with the ribs."

She started the CD player again before sitting down with her tray in her lap, hoping the lovely Christmas music with its message of God's love would calm their spirits. They ate in silence as the music played. When they finished eating, Sylvia carried the trays back into the kitchen.

"Good lunch. Thanks. No special projects for this afternoon?"

She caused a smile to dance at her lips. "Of course, I have a project! A relaxing one I think you'll enjoy. On and off this past year, I've been working on our family scrapbooks, mounting many of those pictures we've been tossing into that big drawer all these years. I thought you might like to take a look at them." She was pleased when he gave her an enthusiastic smile. After taking three scrapbooks from the shelf and placing them on the coffee table, she sat down by Randy and opened the one on top. "This first one starts the year we began dating. Look at this funny picture of the two of us on that parade float. Can you believe we ever agreed to wear those silly costumes?"

He leaned in for a better look. "You were a real looker. No wonder I fell for you."

"Well, you were quite handsome yourself. All the girls thought so."

He flipped the page and pointed to a photo in the top corner. "I'd nearly forgotten about that old bicycle. I wonder what ever happened to it."

She leaned into him with a giggle. "Remember how you

used to ride it backwards? I could never figure out how you did that."

"Oh, look, here's a picture of my mom in that old car my dad had."

"And here's another one of the two of us paddling that old canoe we rented at the boathouse."

Randy let out a raucous laugh. "As I recall, you lost hold of your paddle and turned us over when you tried to reach for it."

She punched his shoulder playfully. "Me? I wasn't the one who lost that paddle; it was you, Randy Benson! You turned us over!"

"Oh, there's a picture of Buddy Gilbert. Remember him? He spent more time in the principal's office than he did in the classroom. That kid was always in trouble."

She flipped over several pages and pointed to a full-page picture of the two of them, taken after their wedding by the photographer. "We made a handsome couple, didn't we? Look how happy we were. I was so excited about being Mrs. Randy Benson, I couldn't get the smile off my face. I felt like a fairy princess in that dress. And look at that flashy tuxedo you were wearing. What a handsome groom you were."

"I'll never forget how beautiful you looked in that dress."

Her pulse quickened. "I—I don't want you to forget, Randy."

The lines bracketing his mouth tightened, and she wondered if, once again, she had gone too far. "Do you have any of Buck's baby pictures in here?"

She flipped a couple more pages, then pointed to the picture of a preemie wearing the funny little hat they put on tiny newborns. "He's only a few hours old in that picture. Can you believe that tiny baby is now over six feet tall and extremely healthy? God did a miracle in his life."

Randy gazed at the picture, touching it with his fingertips.

"I was so scared, Syl. I was so afraid we'd lose him."

She carefully leaned her head onto his shoulder, hoping and praying he would not push her away. "Me, too. I knew how much you wanted a son."

"And now we have two sons."

"And DeeDee." She sat up and flipped another page. "Look, there's a picture of our twins. So many of the nurses remarked how cute they were. Nothing skinny about those two."

"I expected you to have a hard delivery when the doctor told us how big they were. Look at Aaron's fist! That boy came out ready to do battle."

"Aaron has always reminded me more of you than Buck. He and DeeDee both have your coloring and your dark, curly hair. Buck is more like me."

Randy took her hand and gave it a pat. "He not only looks more like you, he has your same patience and disposition. Lucky kid!"

"Here, I want you to see the pictures we took that time we all went on vacation to Branson, Missouri." She flipped a few more pages.

"What a trip that was. Why did we ever decide to camp out in that big tent rather than stay at a motel? It rained every day we were there."

She let out a giggle at the thought. "Everything we owned was drenched. As I remember, that tent molded before it dried out, and we had to throw it away. Your idea of camping out wasn't such a good idea after all, but the kids had fun."

He reared back. "My idea of camping? It was your idea."

"But you're the one who always talked about the fun you had camping out when you were a boy!"

"In the backyard! If it rained, all I had to do was grab my pillow and blanket and go in the house."

Sylvia planted her hands on her hips. "I never wanted to

camp out. I only suggested it because you had talked about it so much. I never realized you'd only done it in your backyard!"

"I guess the joke was on both of us."

They went through all three albums, reminiscing with each page, laughing, sometimes crying, sometimes just remaining silent, and enjoying their memories. So many times, Sylvia thought Randy was on the brink of saying something, especially when she could see tears in his eyes. Sometimes she thought she saw a flicker of love, but he remained silent. Close to her at times. Withdrawn at other times.

"Our twenty-five years might not have been perfect, Randy, but they were ours. Yours and mine. We created a life together because we loved one another and wanted to spend our years together. I've never once been sorry I said 'I do,' and I've never stopped loving you, and I never will, no matter what happens."

"Syl—"

"Don't say it, sweetheart. I know you don't want to hear that right now, but I have to let you know how I feel." She motioned toward his recliner. "Why don't you take a little nap while I fix dinner? I'll wake you when we're ready to eat."

"I can help—"

Deciding her emotions had already been yanked around enough for one day and needing a few private minutes to herself, she held up a palm. "Not this time, Randy. Rest."

"But—"

"Please. Let's do this my way, okay?"

She hurried into the kitchen and checked the oven. The beef roast she had put in to bake that morning was just right. She scurried into the dining room, put her lace tablecloth on the table, and set it with her most delicate china and silverware. In the center of the table, she put a fresh pine candle ring, the one she and Randy had purchased at the YMCA lot when they had bought their Christmas tree, and added a big, fat red candle in the center. She lit the candle and stood back, admiring its beauty, then lit the candelabras on the highly polished buffet, giving the entire room a soft, romantic glow.

Once the gravy was made, the potatoes and carrots put into their serving bowls, squares of homemade cranberry salad placed on lettuce leaves, and the corn bread browned just right and everything placed on the table, she removed her apron, checked her appearance in the pantry mirror, and went into the family room to awaken her husband.

"I couldn't sleep," he told her as she came into the room. "I've been thinking about all those pictures you've put in those albums. It must've taken you weeks to arrange them like that and add all those notes under each photograph."

"Give her of the fruit of her hands; and let her own works praise her in the gates." She grabbed his hand and tugged him to his feet with an inward smile as she remembered the verse the Lord had given her. "Like most of the things I do, Randy, it was a labor of love. Come on. Dinner's ready."

He stopped at the archway leading into the dining room, his eyes wide. "Wow, you're going all out. Is that round thing what we bought when we got the Christmas tree? That thing around the candle?"

She moved to her place at the table, pleased that he noticed it. "Yes, do you like it? It smells wonderful. It's bayberry."

He hurried around the table and pushed her chair in as she sat down, then moved to his own seat. "Umm, brown gravy."

"I—I thought maybe—rather than having one of us pray— we might recite the Lord's Prayer together."

"If you want to."

She bowed her head and closed her eyes, folding her hands in her lap. "Our Father, which art in heaven." She paused, but not hearing Randy, went on. Eventually, he joined in with her, but she could tell there was no enthusiasm in his tone, and she almost wished she had not suggested it. "For thine is the kingdom and the power and the glory forever. Amen."

"This is nice, the two of us eating in the dining room like this." He heaped a huge helping of mashed potatoes on his plate, then reached for the gravy boat. "We should've done this more often."

"I tried a number of times, even had the table set and a special meal fixed, but then something would happen at the newspaper, a press would quit working, a paper delivery didn't show up on time, or some other catastrophe would happen, and you'd call and say you weren't going to make it home for dinner."

His face grew serious. "I'm sorry, Syl, I didn't know. You never complained about it."

"I didn't want to add to your problems. You had enough to take care of."

"Guess you haven't been too happy these past few years, either."

She shook her head vigorously. She had to make him understand. "That's not true! I *have* been happy. However, I would have been happier if you and I could've had more time together; but I understood, sweetheart. Honest I did! I knew you would've preferred being home with your family—" She drew in a deep breath as visions of Randy asking her for a divorce on Thanksgiving Day came back to haunt her. "Or— or at least I thought you would."

"I—I used to want that, but I never realized you did, too. You seemed to have more interest in the family cat than you did me. I've felt like an outsider in my own home for more times than I can remember, Syl. You shut me out. You *and* the kids. Sometimes I felt like none of you cared if I lived or died, as long as the paycheck continued."

She bristled. "That's a rotten thing to say, Randy Benson!

I'm just glad the children aren't here to hear you make such a ridiculous statement! Do you have any idea how that makes me feel? Or do you even care about my feelings?" She swallowed hard and let out a long, low breath of air as she glanced at her watch. "We have to stop this. We only have three hours until midnight. I want those three hours to be pleasant, not a shouting match."

He nodded but did not look at her, just moved his carrots around on his plate.

"How's the roast?"

He raised his head slightly and gave her a weak smile. "Perfect. Best I've ever had. You're a terrific cook."

"Thank you." Sylvia tried to appear calm on the outside, but inside she was seething. *Why did I let him bait me like that? I wanted this evening to be perfect, one that would make Randy see what he was giving up if he left me, and what did I do? Nagged at him like some cartoon figure! Three hours! Lord, what shall I do? I'm all out of ideas. I felt sure that once Randy spent this week in our home, being reminded of the vows we took and the lives we've lived for the past twenty-five years, he'd want to come home. But now—I'm wondering if he, too, is counting the minutes until midnight—so he can get out of here, away from me!* She could not stop them. Tears flooded down her cheeks like a sudden rainstorm on a spring day.

Randy noticed and, hurrying around the table, put his arm about her. "Syl, are you okay? Aren't you feeling well?"

She turned away from him and got up from her chair. "I'm sorry, Randy. I never meant to spoil our evening. Give me a few minutes, okay? I'll be fine. Finish your dinner." With that, she rushed from the room and up the stairs, seeking the solitude of their bedroom.

≈

Randy stood by, helplessly watching her leave the room. *Randy, old boy, that was some smooth move. Are you so concerned about how you feel that you've forgotten other people have feelings, too?*

He sat back down and tried to eat, but the guilt he felt for mouthing off made the food wad up in his stomach. Sylvia had been nothing but kind to him all week, going out of her way to prepare the foods she knew he liked, taking him to places he hadn't been in years, and doing so many other things.

He placed his fork on his plate and leaned back in the chair, staring into the flame of the candle. She didn't deserve this kind of treatment, yet what else could he do? It was not fair to get her hopes up. Their marriage was over. Had been for years, as far as he was concerned. She did not care about him. Not really. Otherwise, she would have realized how he felt long ago. She would have changed and done something about it.

She would have changed? She would have done something about it? That still, small voice said from deep within his heart. *What about you? Did you make any attempt to change into the man she wanted you to be? Did you once even consider her happiness, as well as your own? Don't let these last three hours slip by. This is Christmas Day, Randy. You're not a selfish man. Surely, one day of the year you can put Sylvia first and forget about yourself.*

"I'm sorry, Randy. Please forgive me."

He turned to see Sylvia standing in the archway, and she was smiling. "Nothing to forgive, Syl. I was as much to blame as you, maybe more."

She reached out her hand as she moved toward him. "Can we start the evening over?"

He took her hand, lifted it to his lips, and kissed it. "I'd like that."

Once they were seated, Sylvia picked up the platter of corn

bread and passed it to him. "It's kinda cold now. I could heat it for you."

He took it from her hands with a genuine smile. "It's fine, Syl, just like it is."

The rest of the meal was pleasant as each of the Bensons went out of their way to avoid confrontation or any mention of the divorce. "Would you like to wait a bit before having dessert?" she asked him when they had finished. "Later, in the family room with another cup of coffee?"

"Sounds good to me." He rose quickly. "Let me help you with the cleanup."

"I don't want to waste a minute of the few hours we have left," she told him as she picked up the roast platter. "I'm going to put things in the refrigerator and leave the dishes until later." They carried things to the kitchen, placing the dirty dishes in the sink, then headed back to the family room.

❧

"Sit by me, Randy." Sylvia patted the sofa cushion beside her.

He glanced at his watch, then stood gazing at her for a few moments before moving to her side and resting his head on the sofa's high back. "Sure hope the kids made it to Colorado okay."

Scooting a tad closer to him, she leaned her head on his shoulder, taking in his nearness, the smell of him, and the slight sound of his breathing. No matter what the future held, she wanted to capture this moment forever in her memory. She and her beloved, sitting close to one another, watching the lights twinkle merrily on the tree, listening to Christmas music extolling their Savior's birth. Would there be more nights like this, or would this be the last one?

Taking her hand in his, he caressed it with his thumb, causing her heart to do a flip-flop. Even after all these years, just his touch made her tremble.

"Are you cold?" Randy slipped an arm about her shoulders and pulled her to him. "That better?"

She nodded and snuggled up close. She wanted so much to tell him how she loved him, how much she wanted him to stay, but the words would not come. *Maybe you've said too much already, My child.* She flinched as the still, small voice spoke from deep within her heart.

But, God, I have so little time left! I have to make Randy see how important it is that we stay together as husband and wife!

Perhaps, if you'd worked as hard at trying to please Randy these past few years as you have this week, he wouldn't have considered leaving you, the voice answered in a kind way. *Yes, raising your children was important; it was a job I called you to do. And all the things you did for other people, to please and serve Me, were important, too, but not at the cost of putting your husband last.*

I—I never meant to put him last, and part of it was his fault. He was always so busy—

And you weren't? the small voice asked.

Yes, I was busy. Too busy. However, I can't take the whole blame. What about that woman? That Chatalaine person?

"Syl, are you sure you're not coming down with a cold or something?" Randy asked.

His voice pulled her from her thoughts. "A cold? No, I— I don't think so, I'm just—just, well, you know. It's nearly midnight."

He checked his watch again. "I know."

Pressing back tears, she forced a smile and jumped to her feet. "Why don't I fix us some hot cocoa? Doesn't that sound good? With marshmallows on top like we used to fix for the kids."

He gave her the sideways grin she always loved. "Only if we can have some of those cookies we baked to go with it."

"You got it!" She gave him her sweetest smile and hurried

into the kitchen, hoping to regain her composure. A few minutes later, she was back with the tray, setting it on the coffee table in front of them.

"Here ya go!"

They enjoyed their treat while talking about their children and Christmases past. Though Sylvia chattered on happily, panic was clutching its fingers tightly about her throat, and a jagged piece of her heart was breaking off with each stroke of the second hand on the clock. There was nothing in Randy's speech or demeanor that gave even the slightest indication he planned to stay beyond midnight. *Is he wondering about Chatalaine? Where she is and what she is doing? Oh, God, please, no! Don't let that woman break up our marriage! I love him so! I need him! My family needs him!*

Finally, Randy stood and walked to the hall closet, pulling something from his coat pocket. "I have something for you." He lowered himself back down beside her, holding a small, beautifully wrapped package in his hand. "It's actually my Christmas present to you, but I felt funny giving it to you Christmas Eve with everyone there. I—I decided I'd rather give it to you in private."

Feelings of joy and happiness flooded over Sylvia as he placed the package in her lap. Halting a compelling urge to weep, she carefully pulled off the paper, making sure not to tear it, revealing a square white box. She smiled up at Randy, both pleased and relieved he had actually bought a gift for her. It did not matter what it was. She would have been happy with the empty box, just knowing he had not forgotten her after all.

"Open it." He took the wrappings from her hand and placed them on the table.

Inside, was a deep blue velvet box. Her hands shook as she lifted the lid and gasped. "Oh, Randy!"

"It's the diamond heart necklace I always said I'd buy you but couldn't afford. Like the one we saw in the jewelry store window, remember? The store where I bought your gold wedding band." He lowered his head sheepishly. "I—I should have bought it for you years ago."

Sylvia was so deeply touched, she could barely breathe as she stared at the spectacular necklace. They had joked about it for years, but she had never actually expected him to buy it for her. "Oh, Randy, I love it. It's so—so beautiful! Are you sure—"

He took the box from her hands, removed the necklace from its bed of white velvet, and opened the clasp. "Here, turn a bit and let me fasten it on you."

As she turned, she heard the clock on the fireplace chime a single chime. *Eleven thirty!*

"There!" Randy said, leaning forward to admire the necklace. "You look as beautiful in it as I knew you would."

"Does—does—" She lifted watery eyes to his, her voice raw and shaky with emotion as she fingered the necklace. "Does this mean you're staying?"

Randy looked into her eyes for some time before he answered. "No, Syl, that necklace is not only a Christmas present; it's my going-away gift." He glanced quickly at his watch, then said without preamble, "I—I'll be leaving at midnight."

Sylvia grabbed onto his arm, tears of humiliation and hurt blurring her vision. "No, Randy, no!"

His hand covered hers as her world tilted off its axis. "This week has been wonderful—I won't deny it, but there's no going back, Syl. I think we both know that. Our marriage has been on the skids for a long time. One week together, taking a walk down memory lane, could not resurrect it. Let's face it. It's dead and ready to be buried."

"But, Randy, there's more at stake here than you and me! What about our children?"

He blinked hard, then looked away, as if he didn't want her to see how this thing, this giant that was tearing them apart, was affecting him more than he'd admit. "They'll recover."

"They won't, Randy," she said, sounding stronger and more rational than she had dreamed possible. "Don't expect them to understand, because they won't."

"I'll—I'll have to deal with that. Try to make them understand. We're not the first couple to divorce. Over fifty percent—"

"Don't try to excuse this by quoting statistics! Do you think God will accept your statistics as an excuse when you stand before Him?" She grabbed onto his chin, forcing him to look at her. "You're a Christian, Randy! You know this is displeasing to God!"

He shrugged but did not pull away. "Lots of things are displeasing to God, Syl. Not just divorce."

She tried to find a snappy retort, some scripture she could quote to him to prove he was in the wrong, but her mind went blank.

Randy reached up and slowly pulled her hands from his face. "I'm sorry, Syl. Honest, I am. I've struggled with this thing for the past two years; now it's time for action. I have to try my wings. I know it'll take time, but I'm hoping, eventually, we can at least be civil to one another—for our children's sake. After all, we managed to spend this week together."

"Only because I thought there was hope for us." Sylvia shot a quick glance at the clock. One minute to midnight.

"You promised, Syl. One week with you, and if I still felt the same way, you would give me the divorce—uncontested. You are going to keep your word, aren't you?" he asked softly, as if he expected her to go into a rage and back out on her deal, maybe even take a swing at him.

She had no choice. She'd done her best to try to get Randy to change his mind, and despite the many times she thought he was being swayed during their week together, he was as determined as ever to go through with the divorce. To go back on her word now would only make her look foolish and like a liar. Stunned and shaken and assailed with emotion, she stood to her feet. "I won't back out. I did give you my word, but I want you to remember one thing. I never wanted our marriage to end this way. I love you, Randy. I'll always love you."

He took her hand and held onto it tightly for a moment, then backed away.

"Not so fast. I still have fifteen seconds. I have one more request."

His brows rose in question.

"Hold me, Randy. Kiss me good-bye like you used to when we were young and so much in love nothing else mattered."

"But—"

"Time is getting away—"

He stepped forward awkwardly and pulled her into his embrace, his lips seeking hers. To her surprise, his kiss was warm, passionate, and lingering as he pulled her so close it took her breath away and their kiss deepened.

As the clock chimed midnight, he pulled away and walked out of her life.

Sylvia watched him go through that door and close it on twenty-five years of marriage. She wanted to die.

twelve

The next few days were the saddest days Sylvia had ever spent as she closed herself up in the house, keeping the shades drawn to shut out the sunlight.

DeeDee and Aaron were still gone. Buck and Shonna had visiting relatives at their house and were only able to spend a little time with her. They had invited her to come to their home, but she did not feel up to it and certainly not up to putting on a happy face and visiting with strangers.

And, worst of all, the God she loved and trusted had not answered her prayers. He, too, had forsaken her, just like Randy. She had never felt so all alone. In less than two days, she devoured the two-pound box of chocolates Buck and Shonna had given her for Christmas. Good, nourishing food remained in the refrigerator. She had no interest in it whatsoever. Chocolate was the only thing that seemed to satisfy. She did not want to talk to anyone, not even Jen, and especially not God!

Television held no interest, not even the Sky Angel Christian channel with its twenty-four hours of music, preaching, and talk shows.

She leaped to the window at the sound of every car going down the street, sure it was Randy coming back to tell her the whole thing had been a mistake or a bad joke that went too far.

She grabbed up the phone each time it rang, hoping to hear his voice. But it was never Randy. She even screamed into the phone at the next telemarketer who called, threatening to report him if he ever called her again, which was definitely not her true nature.

Each day, she rushed to the mailbox hoping to find a letter from Randy or a card, even a simple note, but none ever came.

She wanted desperately to call him, to beg him to come back to her, to give her another chance to show him how much she loved him and wanted their marriage to succeed. She wanted to tell him she was even willing to forgive his infidelity and would never mention it to him again. But then, just the thought of Randy and that woman together made her want to throw up, and she knew how hard it would be to keep that promise.

But what if Randy had been telling her the truth about Chatalaine? That there really hadn't been anything between them? As far as she knew, he had not made a single attempt to call the woman during the entire week. How would she have felt if Randy had falsely accused her of cheating on him, and she had been innocent? The thought struck horror to her heart. Could Randy have been telling the truth all along? Had he really simply been tired of being married to her as he had said? And wanted out? And there had never even been a relationship with Chatalaine?

No, she could not call him, not even to tell him she forgave him. A call from her, after he had finally made his move and walked out on her, would only anger him, especially if Chatalaine was there at the office with him. She glanced at the phone. It was so tempting to call, but she turned away.

Jen phoned several times, but Sylvia always ended their conversation as quickly as possible without being rude, leaving her friend to wonder how she really was. She had even refused Jen's offer to pray for her. Why should anyone pray for her? God did not care about her. If He had, He would have brought Randy to his senses and healed their marriage. *No, prayer doesn't change anything*, she told herself as she shoved her Bible into the drawer with plans to leave it there. *No more daily Bible reading—no more praying for me. If God were real, He would have shown Himself and kept Randy here where he belonged.*

Late the afternoon of the thirtieth of December, the doorbell rang, and Sylvia rushed to answer it.

"Are you Sylvia Benson?" the man standing at the door asked.

She nodded. "Yes, that's me."

"This is for you." He handed her a plain-looking envelope and, without another word, hurried to his car and drove off.

She carried it into the house, tearing it open on the way. As she pulled the paper aside, she let out a loud gasp and collapsed onto the sofa, one hand resting on her forehead, her heart beating fitfully. *These are the divorce papers Randy had said would be coming!* After taking several restorative breaths to calm herself, she lifted the pack of papers and read the first few lines. "Oh, Randy, how could you? I never thought you would actually go through with it, especially this soon. Not until you'd had a chance to tell the children!" She tossed the papers aside, too weak and too wounded to read another word. "God," she called out shaking her trembling fist. "Why—why have You forsaken me?"

She wandered about the house aimlessly, not knowing what to do or where to turn. Should she call Buck? Tell him about the divorce papers? What good would it do? There was nothing he could do to help her other than hold her hand to console her. He and Shonna had a house full of relatives. It would not be fair to her son and his wife to upset them at a time like this. Especially since Shonna was pregnant. She could just imagine the happiness and festivities going on at Buck's house as he and Shonna shared their good news with her parents and aunts and uncles. No, she could not do anything to take away from their joy.

She skipped supper, barely remembering she should eat, and went to bed early, pulling the covers over her head, touching the pillow where, only a few days ago, Randy had laid his head. Just the thought of his never being there again sent her into wild hysterics of crying until her eyes were so red and swollen, she could barely open them.

The next morning, Jen phoned again, this time trying to talk Sylvia into coming to the New Year's Eve service at the church. "You can't lock yourself away like this, Sylvia. It's not good for you."

"Not good for me, Jen? What *is* good for me?" she spat into the phone. "I don't think any of my church friends want me crying on their shoulders—the poor little woman whose husband left her for another woman because he didn't want to be married to her anymore."

"That's not true, sweetie. Your church family cares about you. You are not the first person whose marriage ended in this way. You didn't want your marriage to break up. You were the innocent partner."

Sylvia grasped onto the phone tightly, her knuckles turning white. "You're wrong about that, Jen. There was nothing innocent about me. Stupid, maybe, but not innocent. I see that now. Even if that woman hadn't come along, our marriage wouldn't have lasted. I—I put Randy last in my life. Behind our children, the church, my activities. I was never there when he needed me. It took our week together for me to realize that. If only I could go back and do things over."

"Well," Jen drawled out, as if not knowing what else to say,

"I'm praying that you'll come tonight. I'm sure you need God and the church more than you're admitting. We all need Him, Sylvia. If you don't want to have to talk to anyone, sneak in after the service starts and sit in back. You can even leave a few minutes before midnight, if you want. Just come, though. Start the New Year out right."

"Don't waste your time watching for me, because I probably won't be there."

As Sylvia hung up the phone and gazed about the room, Jen's words drilled into her heart. *I'm sure you need God and the church more than you're admitting.* She shrugged as she pulled her robe tighter about her and settled down in Randy's chair to finish her cup of cold coffee, idly picking up the remote and hitting the ON button.

"You may think no one loves you, no one cares what happens to you, but God cares," a gray-haired man with a kind face was saying as the Sky Angel channel lit up the screen. "Oh, He isn't some magical genie who snaps into being when you summon Him, eager to grant your every wish. However, He has a plan for you. A plan to prosper you and not harm you."

Her ears perked up, and she began to listen in earnest. *That's the very verse Randy quoted!*

"God has engraved you on the palms of His hands. His plan for you is perfect. Oh, at times it may seem like He's not listening when you call out to Him. Even as a born-again Christian, you may feel praying is a useless thing. Sometimes, you may have doubts about His existence and even wonder if there is a God. Satan puts those doubts in your mind. You must not let him have the victory."

Sylvia leaned forward with rapt attention.

"We who are Christians and claim His name must always remember," the preacher continued, "God has His own timing for everything. Only in His appointed time will He bring things to pass. All we can do is wait upon Him, pray, and seek His will. If you are listening to my voice right now and you feel God has forsaken you, it's time to give up your pity party and start living again. Seek God's face. Confess your sins. Turn to Him. Trust Him. His plan is always best for you."

Sylvia stared at the screen. It was as though the man was speaking directly to her. *I have been having a pity party! It's time I faced up to the fact that I have done everything I could to save our marriage and I failed. It's time I turned it all over to God. My life. Randy's life. If God cannot put things back together, no one can!*

She glanced about the darkened room. Dozens of the little fluted white papers that separated the chocolates she had consumed lay scattered about the floor. Empty coffee cups adorned the coffee table. Tissues she had used to wipe at her eyes and blot her nose were strewn everywhere. Two days! She had two days to get things back in order before DeeDee and Aaron came back from their skiing trip. She could not let them come home to the house in such disarray. It was going to be bad enough to learn their father had left their mother and had served her with divorce papers.

Putting her sorrow and heartache aside, she flung open the drapes, lifted the blinds, gathered up the trash, cups, and dishes, putting them in their proper places. The kitchen was still a mess from the dirty dishes, pots, and pans she had left on the cabinet and in the sink the night Randy had left. Rolling up the sleeves on her robe, she dove into the mess with zest and soon had the kitchen looking the way she usually kept it—spotless. She ran the sweeper in the family room, leaving the tree standing in the corner, waiting for either Buck or Aaron to help her get it out of its stand and to the curb where the trash man would pick it up. She dusted and waxed until the whole downstairs shone.

Next, she hurried upstairs, changed the sheets on the bed in their bedroom, even scooting the bed to a different wall to give the room a renewed look.

By eight o'clock, after eating a bowl of soup, she was in the shower with plans to attend the New Year's Eve service. The cool water falling onto her face from the showerhead was invigorating, and she knew, though life was going to be hard in the coming days, she would make it. She still had her health, a beautiful home, a terrific bunch of kids, her church friends, and, most importantly, God. Granted, she and God's relationship was a bit strained, but in time, she knew He would soften her heart and the two of them would be on good terms again. She knew now—she had left God—He had not left her.

She slipped into the service shortly after ten o'clock, just after the song service had begun, and took a seat way in the back in an empty area under the balcony. Thankfully, the lights in the sanctuary were turned low since candles burned in the candelabra on either side of the pulpit. Her gaze went to the third row from the front on the left side of the sanctuary, the row where she and Randy sat when he wasn't too busy at the paper to attend church. She would have to find another pew to sit in on Sunday mornings. That one held too many memories. Maybe she would just sit with Jen from now on. She always sat alone or with one of the widow women since her husband was always up on the platform preaching.

The song service was wonderful, as was the special music. It was as though all the worship team's songs had been chosen with her and her needs in mind. When the pastor asked for those who wanted to give a testimony of what God had done for them this past year, at least a dozen people responded. As Sylvia listened to their words, her own problems seemed to fade. With some, the Lord had brought them through a life-threatening disease. With others, an injury—one that had robbed them of a way to support their families, but God had been faithful and supplied their needs. With one family, it was the loss of a child through an accident. One couple's marriage had been ripped apart by infidelity. However, through confession of sin, apologies, forgiveness, and God's grace, the family had been reunited and was happier than ever. Each story was different, yet each ended with victory through the Lord Jesus Christ.

Sylvia didn't even try to keep the tears from flowing as she listened. Their stories were like a soothing salve on her troubled mind. If they could make it, surely she could.

The pastor's New Year's message was exactly what she needed to hear as he spoke about putting old things aside and beginning things anew. He talked about restoration with God and renewing your joy in Jesus. He even encouraged making New Year's resolutions, not in the way the world makes them, but as goals we should set to make us the people God would have us to be. Goals like daily Bible reading and prayer and serving Him.

A few minutes before midnight, the pastor invited anyone who wanted to pray the New Year in to come forward and kneel at the altar. Sylvia watched as a number of parishioners stood and moved forward. This was the time she had planned to duck out and leave. However, as she stood, to her surprise and dismay, her feet led her forward, and she found herself walking toward the altar. She no longer cared if anyone saw her tears or realized she would soon join the ranks of the divorced people who attended the church. All she had on her mind was getting to that altar, kneeling, asking God's forgiveness for ever doubting Him, and turning her life over to Him.

When she reached the front, she immediately dropped to her knees, folding her hands and resting them on the curtained railing. With a broken and contrite heart, she began to pray silently, talking to God, spilling out her heart to Him in Jesus' name.

As she prayed, she felt a hand on her shoulder. Without even needing to glance back, she knew it was Jen. She continued to pray, thankful for such a good friend. Remembering the pastor's challenge, she let her tears of surrender flow down her cheeks, her heart filled with gratitude to God for the many blessings He'd given her throughout her life and for the blessings He'd promised in His Word to continue to pour upon her. *I am not much, Father, and I have made so many mistakes, but take me, use me, mold me into whatever You want me to be.*

"I love you," a male voice whispered softly in her ear.

Startled, since she had assumed it was Jen who had kneeled beside her, she turned quickly toward the voice. "Ra–Randy? What are you doing here?"

His cheeks stained with tears, he warily slipped an arm about her, whispering, "Although you and I have grown apart over the past few years, Sylvia, I want you to know there has never been anyone in my life but you. I have so missed the closeness we used to have. You were always so wrapped up in our children's lives—I guess I was jealous of the time you spent with them."

She rubbed at her eyes with her sleeve. "Jealous of our children?"

He nodded, wiping at his own eyes. "I—I was so busy at the newspaper, we never had time for each other. I have acted like the typical midlife-crisis male and let my ego cloud my judgment. I responded like the old fool that I am, wanting to move out and find myself. I knew better, Sylvia. I knew I was going against God's will. Looking back, I cannot imagine how I ever let myself try to put the blame for our failed marriage on you. But thanks to you and our one last Christmas together, I now see what a fool I have been. I didn't fully realize what a mistake I was making until I got back to my apartment after leaving you that last night we had together. I have been miserable ever since. Spending the week with you and realizing what I was about to give up made me see things in a new light, but I was too proud to admit it."

"But—but the divorce papers! They were delivered to me just yesterday."

He scrunched up his face and drew in a deep breath. "I didn't know my attorney was going to have them delivered that soon. I was sick about it when he told me. What that must have done to you! I'm so sorry, Syl."

"But—but what about Chatalaine? What are you going to do about her?"

"I—I know you don't believe me about Chatalaine, but sweetheart, honest, there never has been anything going on between us. You can talk to her if you want and ask her yourself. We're both invited to her wedding next week."

Sylvia's jaw dropped. "Chatalaine is getting married?"

"Yes. She's been engaged for nearly a year and madly in love with the man she's going to marry, almost as madly in love as I was with you when we were young—and as I am now." He dipped his head shyly. "You're the only woman I've ever loved, Syl. I've asked God's forgiveness for my stupidity."

"But the apricot roses? I thought they were for her. When the florist called—"

"He called you?"

She nodded. "Yes, and he said you'd made a big deal about making sure they were apricot roses when you'd ordered them."

Randy let out a slight chuckle. "And you thought they were for Chatalaine?"

"Who—who else would they be for?"

"Syl, do you remember when we attended old Nick Bodine's funeral last summer?"

"Yes, but what has—"

"I spoke to his wife after the service, and she mentioned Nick had sent her apricot roses on her birthday every year since they'd been married and how much she was going to miss receiving them on her next birthday. I asked her when that was, then wrote it down in my appointment book."

"You sent the apricot roses to Mrs. Bodine?"

"Yes, I always liked Nick. He was a good worker and always had a kind word for everyone. I sent them to her on her birthday, with a note telling her to pretend Nick had sent them to her and to have a Happy Birthday."

Fingering the heart-shaped necklace, she leaned into him, overcome with his thoughtfulness. "Oh, Randy, that was so sweet of you. No wonder you insisted they be apricot roses. I'm sure she loved them."

He slipped his finger beneath her chin and lifted her face to his. "Syl, do—do you think you can ever forgive me for walking out on you like that?" He hugged her tightly to him.

She smiled through tears of happiness and caressed his face with her fingertips as she rested her forehead against his. "Oh yes, my beloved husband. I can forgive you, even as God has forgiven both of us. Despite everything that has happened between us, I have never stopped loving you. I, too, had my priorities all mixed up. While I loved our children and wanted them to have the best lives possible, they were a *product* of our love and not a *substitute* for it. God never meant for them and all the other things in our lives to become a wedge between us. I'm the one who let that happen, and I'm sorry. So sorry, I ever doubted you."

After falling on each other in a loving embrace, they suddenly realized, except for Harrison and Jen, who were sitting on the front pew smiling with happiness, the church was empty. Everyone else had gone. They had been so caught up with each other and their love for one another, they hadn't even noticed.

"You have no idea how excited and happy we are to see the two of you together again," Jen said, her eyes clouded with tears as she hugged both Randy and Sylvia. "We've been praying for you, asking God to bring the two of you back together where you belong."

Randy kept one arm about Sylvia but extended his free hand toward his pastor. "I—I'd like to keep serving on the church board, if you think it'd be okay. That is, if my wife agrees. I'm going to make many changes in my life, but leaving my wife isn't going to be one of them."

He turned to Sylvia, squeezing her hand between the two of his, his eyes filled with tears, his voice cracking with emotion as he spoke. "Would you—could you even consider taking me back? Let me move back home—after what I've done to you?"

Sylvia, too, succumbed to the tears that pleaded to be released. Though he spoke the words she had longed to hear, prayed to hear, she found it difficult to speak. Each heartbeat told her she could trust him. He would never leave her again. "Oh, Randy, of—of course, I'll take you back," she said between sobs of joy. "Spending my life with you is all I've ever wanted." She grabbed onto his shirt collar with both hands and drew him to her, placing a tender, loving kiss on his lips. "Come home with me, darling, where you belong. Where I want you. Where God wants you."

"That's exactly where I want to be."

Sylvia leaned into her husband as Randy kissed her again.

"Hey, you two, break it up," Jen said, rubbing at her eyes and reaching to touch Sylvia's arm. "You're making Harrison and me cry, too."

"Yeah," Harrison added, circling his arm about his wife's waist. "We tough guys aren't supposed to cry."

Randy planted one more quick kiss on Sylvia's lips, then wiped his sleeve across his face. "From now on, I'm setting limits on the time I spend at the newspaper. It's time I get my ducks in a row."

Sylvia let out a giggle at the word *ducks*, as Randy sent her a smile at the little joke only the two of them understood—about his pajamas.

"Of course, we still want you on the board, Randy. You have always been an important part of this church. You're a great asset to us—and to God."

Randy nodded toward their friends. "Well, I'd better get my wife home before she changes her mind. Thanks for caring about us, you two, and for praying for us."

Harrison reached out and gave Randy's hand a hearty shake. "Our pleasure. It's always nice to see God answer prayer and bring a couple back together. Guess I'll see you two sitting in the third row next Sunday morning?"

Randy nodded. "You bet. Right where we belong."

As Randy turned his key in the lock when they reached home, he leaned over and kissed his wife. "Until I spent that week with you, babe, I never realized all the things you did to make our house a home."

"I loved every minute of it." The scripture God had given her the night she had prayed and asked God Himself to give her a plan flooded her memory and gave her cause to thank Him. *"Favour is deceitful, and beauty is vain: but a woman that feareth the Lord, she shall be praised. Give her of the fruit of her hands; and let her own works praise her in the gates."*

Once inside, they walked hand in hand up the stairway and into their bedroom. Randy paused in the doorway, his eyes scanning the area. "You've moved the furniture! I like it this way."

"Moving the furniture is only one of the many changes I plan to make, Randy. Remember what Aaron said Christmas Eve when he was passing out the gifts?"

Randy frowned, as if he was not sure what she meant.

"When he saw the various presents I had given you and acted as though he was upset because he didn't get as many, he said, 'It's okay, Mom. After all, that old man is your husband. He'll be around long after us kids move out for good.' He was right, Randy. It's time you and I began to think of the two of us as a couple and not only as a family. We need to concentrate on us and our needs, as well as those of our children. I want us to do things together, sweetheart. To grow old together."

He gave her a toothy grin. "Will you still love me when we're in a care home and I'm wearing my yellow ducky pajamas?"

"Even then!" She wrapped her arms about his neck and planted a kiss on his lips. "Will you love me when I'm wrinkled and my breasts droop to my waist?"

He laughed, then returned her kiss. "I'll probably be so senile by that time, I won't even notice!"

She tangled her fingers in his hair, much like she'd done when they'd first begun to date. "I hope God grants us many more years together, Randy. We've lost so much time. I want us to make up for it."

"We will, dearest. We've been given a second chance. I want to make the most of it, too."

She leaned into him, enjoying their intimacy. This was where she belonged. In the arms of the man she loved. How close she'd come to losing him—losing everything she held near and dear.

"Syl," he said, his voice taking on a low, throaty, tender quality as he lovingly gazed into her eyes. "Thanks to you and your love and patience with me, this didn't turn out to be our one last Christmas together. I love you, babe."

"I love you, too, Randy."

A Letter To Our Readers

Dear Reader:

In order that we might better contribute to your reading enjoyment, we would appreciate your taking a few minutes to respond to the following questions. We welcome your comments and read each form and letter we receive. When completed, please return to the following:

Fiction Editor
Heartsong Presents
PO Box 719
Uhrichsville, Ohio 44683

1. Did you enjoy reading *One Last Christmas* by Joyce Livingston?
   ❑ Very much! I would like to see more books by this author!
   ❑ Moderately. I would have enjoyed it more if

   _____

   _____

   _____

2. Are you a member of **Heartsong Presents**?   ❑ Yes   ❑ No
   If no, where did you purchase this book? _____

   _____

3. How would you rate, on a scale from 1 (poor) to 5 (superior), the cover design? _____

4. On a scale from 1 (poor) to 10 (superior), please rate the following elements.

   _____ Heroine   _____ Plot
   _____ Hero   _____ Inspirational theme
   _____ Setting   _____ Secondary characters

5. These characters were special because?_____
_____
_____

6. How has this book inspired your life?_____
_____
_____

7. What settings would you like to see covered in future
   Heartsong Presents books? _____
_____
_____

8. What are some inspirational themes you would like to see
   treated in future books? _____
_____
_____

9. Would you be interested in reading other **Heartsong
   Presents** titles? ❏ Yes   ❏ No

10. Please check your age range:
     ❏ Under 18   ❏ 18-24
     ❏ 25-34   ❏ 35-45
     ❏ 46-55   ❏ Over 55

Name _____
Occupation _____
Address _____
City_____ State_____ Zip_____

Presents